FIRST
TIME
SOLO

FIRST TIME SOLO

Iain Maloney

**FREIGHT
BOOKS**

First published June 2014

Freight Books
49-53 Virginia Street
Glasgow, G1 1TS
www.freightbooks.co.uk

A CIP catalogue reference for this book is available from the British Library.

ISBN 978-1-908754-61-5
eISBN 978-1-908754-62-2

Typeset by Freight in Plantin
Printed and bound by Bell and Bain, Glasgow

the publisher acknowledges investment from
Creative Scotland toward the publication of this book

For Minori

'Jazz washes away the dust of everyday life.'
Art Blakey

'I believe in violence. I mean, if you don't believe in violence, you don't go to war.'
Jimmy Maley,
Communist, International Brigade volunteer for Spanish Civil War, POW

'The British Army is not fighting for the old world. If honourable Members opposite think we are going through this in order to keep their Malayan Swamps, they are making a mistake.'
Aneurin Bevan, MP

London. April 1943

I first met Joe on the way to London. The train was quiet and thankfully I'd been left alone. From Invcrayne to Aberdeen, then Edinburgh, changing trains twice, I spoke to no-one. We were pulling out of Edinburgh when Joe burst in, an explosion of swearing I hoped would keep going into the next carriage. Wielding a suitcase that had seen better days and a suit that matched, he made his way towards me, as if something about me was drawing him on. He was short, about my age, but solid as a horse. He'd have made a good rugby player or a boxer, maybe. About 5'3', his hat perched back on his crown, oversize ears, teeth like broken piano keys. His suitcase landed on the luggage rack next to my trumpet case and he crashed down, sweating and out of breath. I watched him over the top of my paper. I'd a copy of the *Melody Maker* with me but had read the same passage three or four times. I pretended to be engrossed. No eye contact, no invitation to start talking. Joe needed no invitation. 'Christ,' he said. 'Very nearly missed it.'

I nodded, acknowledging it appeared that yes, he had nearly missed it, and returned to my paper. 'Aye. I was in some boozer having a last pint and it was further from the station than I thought. I tell you, running with a stomach full of heavy is no a good idea.'

He belched, as if his point needed emphasis. I almost reached for my gas mask. I lit a cigarette to cover the smell. 'Good man,' he said, leaning over and taking one. In my ear, I could hear Lizzie, my sister, saying, 'Tell him where to get off.' I offered him a match.

'So where you going?' he asked. 'London, is it? All the way?'

I nodded. 'Yes, London.'

'Me too. You're no in uniform so I'm guessing you're on your way tae get one. Just turned eighteen then?'

'No, nineteen. Well, at the end of the month.'

Two weeks after my eighteenth birthday I'd signed up. The day of my last exam. Five minutes after 'pens down', a couple of slapped backs, shaken hands and I was through the gates and down the hill, no stopping me on my way to the recruitment office. No Army or Navy for me, though my best mate, Willie Rennie, wanted me to join with him. 'Come on, we'll fight them together, show them what the boys of Inverayne can dae.'

No chance. It was the RAF all the way.

A pilot.

Sharp blue uniform.

Spitfires.

The few.

It's always the pilots that turn a girl's head, and for that you had to volunteer.

My older brother, Dod, had signed up in 1939. He made it as far as France. Dunkirk. Never came back. No room for the dead. No coffin for Dod. French soil for him. Never did find out when or where, just the fact of it. The Chapman boy with a telegram. *Your son. My brother.* I couldn't join the Army, not after Dod. Couldn't let them conscript me. A hole in the sand. Mortars. Dead and buried. I chose the endless sky. Home at the end of the day. A job done. A pint and your grub. Your own bed. Being a younger brother, I had Dod's hindsight. It had to be the RAF.

'Fit wy are ye... I mean, why are you going to London? You're not in uniform either,' I asked. Get my brain in the right gear, keep an eye on my language. What Dod had warned me about. His 'Teuchter' country ways, his 'funny' accent, his inexperience and innocence all marked him out. Knowing how to birth a calf doesn't carry much weight in the city. Speak the King's English and all will be well.

'Fit wy? You're a Teuchter then. Where abouts?'

'Aberdeen,' I said. Inverayne was a fair distance from Aberdeen.

'Aberdeen, aye? I've been up there the once. No a bad wee town. And what's the place there, the ballroom down the beach?'

'The Beach Ballroom?'

'You being funny?'

'No, that's the name.'

'Nice joint. Played a gig there in... '39 I think it was. Aye, just before the war started. You been?'

'No, never. But it's famous. Are you a singer or something?'

'A singer? Me? No fucking chance. Only place you'll catch me singing is at Parkhead... Celtic Fitba Club. Tell me you've heard of them.'

'Aye, yes, kind of. I don't really follow the fit... football.'

'You don't even support Aberdeen?'

'No, not really.'

'They're your local team, boy. You've gottae support the

local team.'

I bit my lip. 'I guess, if I supported anyone I'd support Aberdeen.'

'Fine, so you're a sheep-shagger. Glad we got that straight. I'm a drummer.'

'A drummer? Is that the nickname for a Celtic supporter?'

He laughed hard. 'A drummer,' he said, miming. 'At the Beach Ballroom.'

'Oh, right.'

'That's it? You're only speaking tae the best jazz drummer in Scotland and all you can say is 'oh right'. I suppose if I'd said the accordion I'd have got a better reaction.'

Jazz. The magic word. London was where jazz lived. Dod said there were a lot of dances, a lot of shows put on for the boys. If I could find some others then maybe, just maybe, I could play.

'You all right?' he said.

'Aye, fine. Yes. Is that what you're going to London for? For a gig?'

'Aye, Albert Hall tomorrow night.'

The Royal Albert Hall? To be playing there you really had to be something. 'So how come you're not in uniform?'

'I'm plain clothes,' he said. 'You know. Very hush hush. Hide in open sight. Let's just say I do my bit, and the rest of the time I drum.' I nodded, better not pry. Careless talk and all that. 'So which are you for?' he said.

'Which?'

'Army, Navy or RAF?'

'RAF,' I said, puffing up. 'I'm going to be a pilot.'

'Oh aye,' he said. 'After the fanny, is it?' He laughed. 'Nothing tae be ashamed of. I had the same thought myself back in the day. The birds do love a blue uniform. Then I realised wings wouldnae give me anything I didnae already have. See me? No trouble pulling. Don't suppose you've had more than a sheep or two.'

'Sod off.'

'Ah, he does have some balls after all. I thought you were as wet as the cod they catch in Aberdeen but maybe no. Joe Robertson,' he said, holding out his hand. Despite his stature, his hand was massive. He looked like he could hold his own against Joe Louis.

'Jack Devine,' I said. 'I'm a trumpeter,' I blurted out. We shook. It was the first time I'd met an actual professional jazz musician.

'Any good?' he said.

'I… uh… well…'

'Are you shite or are you being modest?'

'Modest.'

'You dinnae like tae blow your own trumpet?' He stood up. 'Well, Jack the Trumpeter, if you decide that you are any good, we might have a jam sometime. But if you'll excuse me, I'm gonnae see if there's anyone prettier tae talk tae on this train. Hope you get tae be a pilot. Maybe see you around.' He took his suitcase down and moved through to the next carriage. I watched him go, Lizzie commenting in my head: 'That's a right one, right there. Not so much a screw loose as not one properly tightened.'

He must've found someone, as I didn't see him again on the train. We arrived in London early the next morning, my body aching from sleeping upright, my head banging against the window. London, Jack. As far from home as the moon, and just as foreign. Noise, bustle of people. Everything was different. The buildings, the sounds, the voices. Bomb gaps, rubble. No railings, empty signposts. I stood open-mouthed, as I'd warned myself not to. I'd never been further south than Edinburgh, and that was only the once for a series of medical tests and a maths exam to make sure I was physically and mentally fit to become a pilot. What an exam. I hadn't finished it. No-one had. Designed that way. A hundred questions of increasing difficulty. Apparently most people failed and that was that. No RAF for them. The Army or the Navy were the only doors open to those who couldn't manage differential equations. That day I envied Willie. The Army was a piece of piss.

I followed the directions I'd been given to the underground station, showed my pass and traipsed down the stairs deep into the Earth. All very Jules Verne. The Underground. The idea of being on a train under the ground, under the river. I imagined them making it, digging the tunnels, boring through the rocks, the layers, strata, the history of the world stacked. Cambrian, was it? Something else. Silurian. I knew it a year ago. Some of my fellow travellers could also be going to the Air Crew Recruitment Centre. I spotted a pair consulting well-fingered. Maybe I should say hello, I thought, and we could all be lost together.

The ACRC turned out to be Lord's Cricket Ground. We walked through the doors, hundreds of us converging, straightening our backs, squaring our shoulders. A speeded up version of evolution. Men now. All of us men, together. There, to fight. Each born eighteen or nineteen years ago, during the Roaring Twenties, between the wars, when the First World War didn't need a number. My year of waiting was finally over. The RAF were winning. There had been a backlog and I was at the end of the queue. Just wait, was the order. You'll get your chance.

I waited though 1942, a year of disasters, Singapore, Burma, the Philippines. Every evening Da, Lizzie and I sat with the atlas, the wireless and a pencil following the latest developments as they came in. Ma refused to listen. 1942, a year of victories, Midway, El Alamein, Stalingrad. 1942, year of disasters, year of victories, working on the farm, doing more or less what I would've done if there hadn't been a war. While my conscripted classmates left, Willie Rennie and the rest gone, the girls from my year in the WAAF, the ATA, I stayed. I wasn't alone: Murdoch who was more or less blind and James who had a club foot, were still in Inverayne. Everyone knew I wasn't dodging my duty, but while they lived and died with the post, with each sighting of the Chapman boy, here was Jack, safe and sound, coming home every night. It was a slow year. But now London. 1943. My trumpet case swinging, Satchmo's *Basin Street Blues* marking my steps. I was going to fly. I was going to play. I looked around. The suits, the hats, Brylcreem and baggage. Some smoking, some not. Some calmly confident, others looking around for instruction. Some in groups, others solitary. My new friends. Taxiing onto the runway. Goggles on, chocks away.

I found myself beside Terry as we lined up on the cricket field in our civvy suits and overcoats, battered suitcases alongside battered shoes. Split alphabetically into groups – flights, they were called – he and I, Davis and Devine, were together. Terry was tall, with black Brylcreemed hair and a pencil moustache. He looked confident and seemed much older than me, though I was three months older than him. He acted like he was waiting for a bus. I could imagine him leaning against some lamppost on a dark, foggy night tapping a cigarette against his case like Bogart or Grant. That kind of style. A chancer, Lizzie would call him. He spun a coin round his fingers, like a magician, saw me watching. 'It improves dexterity,' he said. 'Good for the cards.'

A gambler. Dod had warned me about this in his letters home. In the forces you have a lot of time to yourself and cards made the time pass. There was always someone who took it too seriously, who couldn't play just for fun. Lizzie warned me as well: 'Don't play, Jackie, you're too easily conned.' Thanks, sis.

'So this pilot is being interviewed by the *Times*,' said Terry, out of nowhere. '"Have you ever been shot down?" asks the interviewer. "Yes, once a Focke shot me down over the Channel. I managed to bail out and got picked up by a fishing trawler." "This was a Focke-Wulf one-ninety?" he asks. "Oh no," he answers. "This fucker was a Messerschmitt."'

A man with a clipboard appeared. We grabbed at the only thing we knew for sure about the military: We saluted him.

'You don't salute a Sergeant.'

He took the register.

'Davis, Terrence?'

'Sir.'

'Devine, Jack?'

'Sir.'

It went on down the line. We practiced drilling, attention, at ease, facing left, right, marched around the field. All our concentration turned on our feet, we forgot what they were for, how to control them. Marching in time meant some had to lengthen their natural stride, others had to shorten it. I was lucky. I had rhythm. Others didn't seem to know the difference between left and right. Slowly the orders got through to us, like a caller at a ceilidh, and our limbs responded. An hour and our feet ached. Order: Inside and form a line at the Medical Officer's room. 'Well, Jack, I hope you've got nothing to hide,' Terry said.

'Why?'

'They're about to check our bits and pieces. Make sure we're clean enough to fly aeroplanes.'

'Clean?'

'Free from infection, Jack. Down there.' He pointed.

'But I've already been checked. After I signed up.'

'Me too,' he said. 'But they're going to check again. You may have been up to no good in the meantime.'

On the farm? Were the others regularly up to no good? I got up to as much no good as I could, which was none at all. The line snaked into the room, a large open space the Medical Officer had set up in. He sat on a chair and the men filed past, dropped their trousers, were examined, redressed and left by a second door. Ahead of us we could hear the comments, laughs and shrieks.

'Call the mess, tell them we've found their missing mushroom.'

'Bloody hell, the length of it, he should be excused shorts.'

'Look at the bend in that! He could do it round corners.'

None of us were long out of school and it was the same changing room humour: Big or small, circumcised or not, no-one got away without judgement being passed. As Terry and I reached the doorway, a round of applause. Curious, we leaned in to see the cause. Even from the back, I recognised the man standing in front of the MO: Joe, hands on his hips, receiving his testimonial. It took me a moment to put everything together. What was Joe doing there? He'd told me he was on his way to play the Royal Albert Hall, that he was 'doing his bit' for the war effort, but he was an Aircraftman Second Class, just like me. There to train to be a pilot, just like me.

It was my turn. Considering the possibilities, I felt I

got off lightly with 'it looks like food's not all that's been rationed.' The next room resembled a large auditorium, a stage at the front and chairs ranked like at a theatre. We were going to be addressed. Joe's group were already seated and we filled the rows behind them. I was two rows back from him, one seat over. I steeled myself, leant across and tapped him on the shoulder. 'Aren't you going to be late for the Albert Hall?' I said.

'Oh, it's you. Jack the Trumpeter.'

'And it's you,' I replied. 'Drummer and spy.'

'What's this?' said the lad next to Joe.

'I met this one on the train down,' Joe said, laughing. 'Spun him a line about being a spy. Swallowed it straight down, so he did. A right Teuchter he is, came in on a turnip truck.'

They laughed, looked back at me, laughed more. I looked to see if Terry was laughing too, but his attention was elsewhere. Officers filed in. A barked order and we were on our feet saluting. By rank, they gave us introductory speeches, varying only in accent and length. The gist was 'do as you're told, keep out of trouble and pass your exams.' Not very rousing. When Dod joined up it was all 'over by Christmas, stick one to Jerry,' upbeat Henry the Fifth crap, but the war had been going for the best part of four years. We didn't need the propaganda: we'd lived the reality. We didn't need priming: we were ready to go. There wasn't a man in the room who hadn't lost someone. Many of us were younger brothers and had been waiting for this day. What we wanted to know was what we'd be doing and when.

The top brass filed back out, leaving us with Sergeant Hawkins, the man we'd mistakenly saluted that morning. 'Right. Over the next few months, here in London and at other postings, you lot will do nothing but drill and study and only if you successfully clear every hurdle, only if you do exactly what is expected, walk the line without deviation, only then will you be allowed anywhere near His Majesty's aircraft.

'This isn't Sunday School. You'll be given no leeway as recruits: Learn the rules, follow them or suffer the consequences. You aren't men yet. You're nothing. My job is to turn you into men. To turn you into RAF officers. We are not interested in what you think or what you hope. You are here to learn how to follow orders without question, how to march, dress, speak and think in one standard fashion. Individuality will not be tolerated. You aren't needed for your creativity or your ingenuity or your intelligence. You are needed because kites can't fly themselves. The RAF doesn't need human beings, it needs machines who follow orders. This is just the beginning of that process. So heads down, mouths shut or you'll never see the inside of a cockpit. Clear?'

Clear enough.

The morning was a blur of orders, shouts, rooms and forms and names. Snatched conversations, brief introductions.

'All right, mate? Seen room 213?'

'Tommy's the name. London born and bred. You?'

'EYES FRONT!'

'Nice suit, pal, how much that set you back?'

'Spare a smoke?'

'QUICK MARCH.'

'Jack.'

'Clive.'

'Micky.'

'Nev.'

'How do?'

By lunchtime I was desperate for a minute to myself. I took advantage of a lull to nip to the toilet, lock myself in a cubicle and just be silent for a minute or two. In my suit, carrying around my suitcase and trumpet, I wasn't part of anything yet. In the afternoon we would get our kit, head to our digs. Maybe once I changed into the uniform, got the cap on, stashed the bag, I'd become an Aircraftman Second Class. Every time we passed in the corridor Joe said something like 'the swan flies south for winter, Mata Hari.' It was just like Dod had said. The next room and the next; lists of rules, facts, figures, statistics. I sat behind a too-small desk trying to fathom the military language on the stack of paper in front of me and thought about my mother's belief that 'school prepares you for life.' I'd thought that meant school taught you how to survive in the world but I was beginning to suspect otherwise. Any time I'd been involved in anything official it featured classrooms, too-small desks and someone shouting. Time blurred, seconds dragged, hours disappeared. That morning's forms were filled, the lectures over. Lunchtime.

The mess, it turned out, was the restaurant at London Zoo. 'Do we get in to see the animals, do you think?' I asked Terry. He shook his head, dipped a chip in his fried egg. 'I've never been to a zoo,' I continued. 'I thocht I might get to see a lion or a giraffe.'

'Thocht?' said a voice from down the table. 'What the 'ell does "thocht" mean?'

'Thought,' I said, reddening.

'Christ, mate,' said the man. 'You don't 'alf speak funny.' The others at the table laughed. 'You a foreigner?'

Now I'd get it. It was like being back at school. In Campbell's class an inadvertent 'aye' could get you the cane. A word like 'thocht' and your hand would be raw for a week. Constant alert, constant vigilance. 'He's Scotch,' said another voice. He'd an accent I couldn't place then, but later learned was Mancunian. 'That's why he speaks funny.'

I kept my head down, tried not to listen. I could imagine Lizzie on her feet, giving them a barrel of anger and a barrel of wit or Willie, his quiet look, 'Outside. Now.' As much as I wanted to, as much as the anger was there, I knew I'd stumble, trip over myself, make things worse. 'You think you two sound normal?' said Terry. We all looked at him. They were as surprised as I that he was coming to my defence. The cockney recovered first.

'More normal than you, you Welsh cunt.'

'Really? Normal for an Englishman would be the King's English. You think you speak like the King?'

'The King's English?' said someone behind me. I turned to see Joe standing with a tray of food. 'That cunt cannae even manage a single sentence. Why would you want tae sound like him? M-m-m-m-m-my l-l-l-l-l-oyal s-s-s-s-s-s-subjects. That's your King whose arse you'd kiss from sunup to sundown and you think "thocht" is funny?' It was a riot. They were on their feet, shouting, threatening. I ducked down, out of harm's way. Terry hardly moved, just his head turning back and forth like it was a sporting event, a football game or something, following the abuse, nodding at a particularly good insult, shaking his head at a weak attack. Blows hadn't been traded yet, but it was only a matter of time.

'If you Jocks hate England so much,' said the one who had laughed at my accent, 'why are you fighting for us?'

'We're no fighting for you,' Joe replied. 'You think we'd die for you and that stuttering cunt of a King?' He couldn't leave it alone. 'We're fighting against Fascism. We're all fighting the Nazis but that doesnae make us all

English, does it? The Yanks and the Russians and the Free
Poles are all fighting the Nazis but does that make them
English? Course no. First we fought Fascism in Spain. Now
we're fighting it across Europe. When that's done we'll fight
Fascism in Britain.'

'There's no Fascism in Britain,' said the same voice.

'Where does Mosley come from? And Lord Haw-Haw?
Half that stuttering cunt's family are Nazis, so they are.'

I wanted out. Joe was dividing us into groups. I said
nothing. I couldn't see, seated in the ring, but officers were
coming. The circle thinned as the spectators retreated.
Everyone had scarpered, leaving Joe, his adversary, Terry
and I, and a few others at the table, staring at our food,
projecting innocence. Joe hadn't noticed. Hawkins let him
go on for a moment more before interrupting. 'So, you're a
Red then, are you Jock?'

'Aye,' he said, wheeling round.

'Sir!'

'Aye, sir.'

'Yes, sir. This is the King's Army and we use his English
here.' I wondered exactly how long Hawkins had been
there. If he'd heard Joe calling King George a cunt, he was
finished. 'Name?'

'Joseph Robertson, sir.'

'Report to me after, Robertson. You're on a punishment
drill for insubordination.'

Joe looked like he was going to say something, but held
it together. The officer waited, his raised eyebrow, sarcastic
smile egging Joe on. Joe was boiling over but he wanted to
be a pilot as much as the rest of us. He kept the lid on. A
nasty grin spread across Hawkins' face.

'We don't like Reds here, Robertson. The Soviets may
be on our side now but we won't forget they were on the

Nazis' side first. Turncoats, each and every man of them. Nazis and Communists? Both scum.'

One slip and he'd be out. Hawkins had made that clear.

Veins twitched. Fists clenched and unclenched. Hawkins left and Joe sat down next to me. The men he'd been arguing with scarpered. Joe said nothing, just started eating.

Orders: Collect kit. Report to digs. We were billeted in requisitioned flats in the area. I looked at the address, at the map I'd been handed, paper flapping around in the wind as I tried to hold it steady without dropping my suitcase of the new kit I was now loaded down with. One of the London boys took charge.

'Follow me, lads,' he said. 'Abbey Road's just round the corner.'

I felt like a pack horse: Suitcase, two kit bags, a back pack, a side pack and a gas mask box. We were supposed to march all the way there, but nobody could manage it carrying all that. Knackered, each coped as best he could. I was used to heavy loads from the farm but Terry, who was also in Abbey Road, was struggling. I wanted to help him. Hawkins, the evil bastard, was watching us, waiting for someone to step out of line. We set off, an unsteady troop. Down the street we turned right. The second we were out of sight of Hawkins our line disintegrated completely. 'Fuck me,' said a voice. 'If I wanted to do heavy lifting I'd have joined the bloody artillery.'

Bags were dropped and rearranged. I helped Terry get his side pack and gas mask box on properly, tightened the straps of his backpack. 'Jesus,' he said. 'Now I know how a snail feels.'

From a side-street, Sergeant Hawkins appeared on a bicycle. The few who noticed snapped to attention. He was purple with rage, though also sporting a smirk of satisfaction. 'What the hell do you lot think you are doing? You are in His Majesty's Royal Air Force now, not your bloody nursery, so you will damn well begin acting like it.'

We leapt back into line at the sound of his voice and a lot of bags were dropped. Lesson learned: Always assume that somewhere there's an officer watching.

Hawkins sent us on our way with an earful of abuse. We continued along Abbey Road, counting down the numbers until we reached ours.

'Bloody hell, boys, this is proper posh.'

High, old buildings, red brick walls, a wide, tree-lined road. Up to then the only posh place I'd ever seen was Inverayne House, seat of the Southalls. Inverayne House stood on the other side of the small forest from our farm. Ma worshipped Lord Southall as a great example of the British gentleman, good manners, always nicely turned out, spoke beautiful English with no hint of an 'aye'. Throughout our childhood we never heard the end of him: 'Do you think Lord Southall acted like that when he was your age?' I was sure he did much worse. We weren't even allowed to use the central doors or the stairs at the flats on Abbey Road. We had to use the 'staff' entrances and the back stairs. The rooms had been cleansed of anything that might resemble luxury. 'I'm amazed they didn't strip out the toilets and replace them with a bucket,' said Terry. Sharing a room with seven others, including Terry. Four sets of bunk-beds jammed into a single bedroom. Where was Willie sleeping? I didn't fancy a hole in the desert. We threw our stuff on our beds and set to unpacking.

'Well,' I said. 'They've at least left the beds and the sheets. I thought we might be camping on the cricket ground.'

'These are nice sheets,' said Terry. 'Worth a bob or two.

I wonder if they'd miss any?'

I tried to unpack as best as I could but there was nowhere to put anything. All throughout the building, all along Abbey Road, all across St. John's Wood, my new comrades, my fellow fliers were doing the same. Hundreds of us unpacking, sorting, changing. Making new friends. Getting into arguments. Pushing kit under beds. I stashed my trumpet out of sight.

Terry had half emptied his suitcase. Cigarettes, chocolate, nylon stockings, a brown paper package, random bags and envelopes were spread out over his sheets. I had the bottom bunk, he the top. It was clearly all black market stuff. I pretended not to notice. A few years back they'd introduced harsh penalties but after years of rations, around us it was business as usual trading potatoes for meat, flour for veg, whatever you had that others wanted. Da swapped milk for whisky. Said it went much better with his tea. Our room-mates also spotted Terry's stash, as I guess he intended, and a discussion of prices started up. It reminded me of the farm: Watching Da haggling over a penny, the disinterested air of the interested man, the semi-aggressive nature of the conversation. A battle. I'd have to do it myself one day, with Dod gone. I couldn't imagine it. Lizzie now, she'd be brilliant. Maybe she could take over the farm. 'How much? For how many grams? Look mate, you may get that in the valleys but you're in London now, you've got to be more realistic. It's a buyer's market here.'

'Fine, go out on the market for your chocolate and nylons, but if you're wanting your hoggins tonight, you'd better get moving.'

'Hoggins? I'd say all that chocolate is for him.'

'And the nylons?'

'Sleep with your backs against the wall, lads.'

We got changed. There was something about the weight of the uniform, the heft of it, the feel of the material that straightened your back, aligned your shoulders. We stood there admiring each other, angling our forage caps this way and that, trying to get the best effect. All fits were an estimate.

'Christ, I'm going to need rubbing with lard to get in and out of these.'

'Stop eating all that chocolate then, tubby.'

'You could fit three of me in this jacket.'

'It's so you can wear it over your parachute.'

I folded my civvy suit away. The uniform was the first clothing I'd ever had that Dod hadn't worn before. I closed my suitcase.

'What's that?' said Terry.

'What's what?'

'That.'

'Oh. It's… it's my trumpet.'

At that moment the cockney who'd been our guide stuck his head around the door. 'All right boys? Settling in? Just spreading the word. There's a boozer round the corner if anyone's thirsty.'

I looked at Terry. 'Pint?'

He shrugged. 'Pint.'

The pub was pretty full when we arrived. I wasn't sure whether to stand at the bar or find a seat, whether to offer to buy a round or just get myself a pint. The only pub I'd ever been in was The Clansman back home, but I knew everyone there. I knew not to sit in Mackie's seat, that the last barstool meant getting up every time Norma needed to collect glasses, that the third table along was wobbly and if you didn't stick a beer mat or two under it your pint would end up in your lap. Terry pushed his way through and ordered two pints of bitter, handing one to me. 'Always get the first one in. Everyone's sober so they remember you buying your round and the group is usually at its smallest so you can save a bit.'

'Cheers,' I said.

'Cheers.' He seemed content to stand at the bar.

'No-one but us RAF boys, by the looks,' I said. 'Makes sense. We're billeted in local flats, so the locals must be elsewhere.'

I'd never met a Welshman before, and his accent was a little hard to follow. A bit Orcadian, but harder, more bass. 'So,' I said, trying to make conversation. 'Wales. What's that like?'

'Like anywhere else, I reckon,' he said. 'Some have, some don't. Some work, some don't. Rain falls down, crops grow up.'

'Any brothers, sisters?'

'Brother.'

'He in the forces?'

'No. Down the pits. Same again.' He gestured with his glass. I took the hint. He was constantly looking past me, over my shoulders, up and down the length of the bar, like he was searching. 'Cheers,' Terry said. 'Back in a bit.' He went over to the hatch at the end of the bar, beckoned the barmaid. Great, I thought. I only know one person and he's buggered off. Everyone around me was deep in conversation. How do you break into a group, join a conversation without being rude, without bringing the chat to a halt? I could stand there waiting for someone to talk to me or I could look busy. There was a paper on the bar. That would do. Now I was alone in a crowded bar, I realised how tired I was. It had been a long couple of days, the goodbyes, Ma crying, Da at the gate, pipe smoke fog, Lizzie walking me to the station all 'have you got your piece?' and 'did you remember your hankie?' playing the nagging mother. Leaving home, the train down, all the marching and paperwork and meeting new people. After that pint I'd head back, I thought, write a quick letter home, get my head down. Tomorrow was bound to be exhausting, and the day after. We were in for a hellish few weeks and we'd have fire-watching night shifts on top. Sleep would be rationed. A body pushed in beside me. Joe.

'All right there. Nobody talking tae you?'

'Just having a look at the news,' I said.

'Dinnae blame you. Right bunch of wankers this lot, I'll tell you. The fuckers I'm bunking with, fairies the lot of them. Service!'

The barmaid was still talking to Terry, so an older bloke I assumed was the landlord came over. 'Pint of heavy, pal.'

'Heavy? Heavy what? Heavy artillery?'

'Heavy what? Speakee English? Heavy, pal. Pint.'

'Listen Chief, I've no idea what you're on about. Now if you want a pint, tell me which beer.'

'Fuck sake, what kind of country is this? No fucking heavy?'

'Oi, Chief, watch the language.'

'Language, fucking aye. What's that piss you're drinking, Jack?'

'Bitter,' I said.

'Fine, pint of bitter.'

The landlord went off shaking his head, muttering. He must get it a lot, I thought. Folk from all over the country. No locals, no regulars anymore. Can't be much fun. I wanted to say something to Joe, 'he's just doing his job', something like that. 'Here you are, Chief.'

Joe took a filthy pound note out, handed it over. The

landlord sighed. 'Got anything else?'

'What you mean, got anything else?'

'Anything that ain't Scotch. These notes are as good as useless down here.'

'What you mean as good as useless? That's a pound that is. See. *I promise to pay the bearer*, pounds sterling, the King's fucking head there, clear as day.'

'Watch the language. I know what it is, we've had enough Scotch through these doors. But I can't circulate it. If you've got any proper money I'll take that.'

'You'll fucking take that or you'll get fucking nothing, pal,' said Joe, his voice rising. Up the bar I saw that Terry had stopped talking to the barmaid. She'd slipped from behind the bar and gone outside.

'I've told you, watch the language. Any more of that and you'll be out.'

'Out? Fucking out? You're gonnae fucking throw me out? I'd like tae fucking see that. I'd like tae fucking see you try, cunt.'

'Right. I warned you. Out.'

'You and whose army?'

I turned and saw the cavalry: The barmaid returned with two policemen. 'Joe,' I said, trying to attract his attention.

'Over here, Bill,' the landlord said to the first bobby.

'Right, son. You heard the man. Out you get.'

'Two of you? You're gonnae need more than two tae make me fucking move.'

'If we need more men we'll call up Sergeant Hawkins and get him down here. Would you like that?'

That made Joe stop. He was in uniform now. 'That's what I thought,' said the bobby. 'Now, let's go.'

'Fucking outrageous, so it is,' said Joe. 'Just trying tae have a quiet pint. It's racialist, so it is. Imperialism. If we werenae Scottish you wouldnae be victimising us like this.'

Us?

Joe necked his pint in one, grabbed his note off the bar. 'Right,' he said to me. 'Let's get out this dump.'

I looked round for help. Terry was too far away. 'Go on,' the landlord said. 'Hop it, and don't come back.'

Joe marched through the crowd, head high. All eyes were on me. Embarrassed, I followed him.

The coppers watched us head down the street. What had just happened? I didn't doing anything wrong. Why pick on me? Joe was laughing.

'Shite boozer anyway. Tomorrow, let's find somewhere better, somewhere with birds.'

He was billeted in the building next to mine. We were supposed to go in the back but Joe ran up the front steps, bold as brass. I watched him from the top of the alley. 'You know, Jack,' he called back. 'They're no better than you. Remember that, right?'

I didn't think they were better than me. I didn't think they were worse. We'd all been enjoying our drinks.

Getting up early was easy for me, fresh from the farm, but others weren't so keen. After breakfast we were back in front of the MO for vaccinations. I was behind Terry again. 'Enjoy last night?' he said.

'Yes, great. Barred from the local for reading the paper.'

'You want to stay away from that one. He's the kind that leaves trails of destruction behind him but walks away fine.'

I was watching the MO. He got through an average of six men before his syringe was too blunt to break the skin and had to change it. I'd either be first or last, depending on my luck. Some men fainted and had to be carried out. 'Aye, well, I didn't invite him over. You buggered off to chat up the barmaid.'

'Betty.'

'Any luck?'

'Not in the way you mean. Purely business.'

'Business? Oh, your... products.'

'Indeed. Are you in need of anything?'

I thought about Lizzie, taking back some chocolate. Maybe Ma would like some. It could be months before I got any leave.

'No, thanks.'

Terry got the new needle, jammy git. Onto the barber, a factory line. Ninety seconds, next.

Classrooms. Desks. Lectures. Marching. Square-bashing, up and down, turning, marching, turning again, being shouted at for a step a second out of time. As we marched I composed ditties in my head to the percussion of our feet. I imagined we were one big jazz orchestra preparing for a concert, like Joe's at the Royal Albert Hall. I was on trumpet, naturally, and as we marched I played my solo to a packed house and received a standing ovation. There'd been no-one to play with in Inverayne and all the time I'd played alone I'd fantasised about being in a band, playing music unscripted, something that grew out of a shared understanding. Organic, totally natural, the world of the farm taught me a great respect for nature. Take one piece away and the world fell apart. The air, the water, the ground, the rocks and trees and plants and insects and cows and worms all contributed to the fertility. I'd gone through the classifieds in the *Melody Maker* and, checking directions with one of the cockneys, had circled a record shop that wasn't too far away. We had the weekends to ourselves and I figured a record shop would be the best place to find out about any gigs going on. I had three weeks in London, and maybe I'd never be back.

In the meantime I composed to the tempo of 140 paces per minute. Sergeant Hawkins assembled us. 'Any complaints?'

Silence. 'No? No-one's got any complaints? I find that hard to believe. Myself, when I was a young recruit like you, my feet were covered in cuts and blisters. Of course in my day you were lucky if your boots fitted. Not like you spoiled lot. Either you are the hardest bunch of recruits we have ever had here or you are all lying.'

Nothing. We weren't biting. 'Now then, lads, I don't want to cast aspersions on your characters but judging by the look of most of you, this is the most physical exercise you have had in quite some time. I know your feet are hurting, so why not admit it?'

Nothing. 'All right then. You are aware that lying to a superior officer is a very serious offence. I know you are, because I told you all this afternoon. By refusing to answer a direct question you are, in effect, lying to a superior officer. Now. Hands up all those with sore feet.'

Slowly, each making sure we weren't alone, hands were raised. 'That's better. A bit of honesty at last. So. All those poor, sore feet. I know a cure for that. A two mile march.'

The classes began. Law, aerodynamics, engineering. Information was thrown at us and if we missed anything, tough. The ditties in my head now had words, formulae and equations, the catechism of Air Force rules recited in time with steadily synchronising boots. Every night before bed, every morning before breakfast, I'd run through what I'd learned. There would be tests, many tests, and I had to pass them all. Another bass drone, constant in my life, like air raids. Coming, coming soon. Joe joined Terry and I for lunch. He'd managed to alienate most of the lads. I'd already heard him referred to as 'that lunatic Jock.' Terry thought he was a lunatic as well, but we couldn't make him piss off without an almighty fight. At first I was on edge, worried he was going to take every sentence the wrong way, kick off for no reason, with me, with anyone, but I only had so much space in my brain. He'd come to my defence, so I gave him the benefit of the doubt. After being tested, prodded, shaved and worked near enough to death, we felt like meat, like beasts whipped around a field. Eating in the zoo seemed fitting. 'The only thing they haven't done to us that they do to these animals is make us impregnate a female of the species while zoology students look on,' said Terry.

'Maybe they're saving that,' I said. 'For after the exams.'

'What, like a reward? Doesn't sound much like a reward to me.'

'Sex?' I said.

'No, doing it in front of a bunch of blokes with lab coats and clipboards. Knowing for sure that she's going to be knocked up at the end of it doesn't sound like much fun.'

'No, I suppose not,' I said.

'You suppose? You've not done it, have you?'

'Shut up, you sod.'

Guffaws around the mess. 'Really? Jesus, at your age. We'll have to do something about that.'

'Listen—'

'No, don't thank me, at least not until it's over.'

Easier to say nothing. I shovelled the food into my mouth. 'What are they feeding the animals?' Joe asked. 'I mean, we're all on rationing. There's never enough tae go around, yet the animals are still here.'

'Not that many of them are,' said a man further down the table. He was tall and well-built, looked like he'd have had a full-head of curly hair had he not shared the same stylist as the rest of us. 'They moved a lot of the big ones out into the country or to Whipsnade and some other zoos.'

'But they must be eating,' said Joe.

'I suppose so,' said the man. 'But most animals are herbivores, so they'll be fine on grass and leaves.' As he spoke he tugged at his collar, like it was too tight.

'Are you telling us,' said Joe, 'that around the country there are lions being kept in fields?'

'I wouldn't have thought so,' he said. 'That would be a bit dangerous. But certainly the non-dangerous ones could be.'

'What about the dangerous ones?' I said. 'Like the snakes?'

'Apparently the really dangerous animals were killed.'

'Good,' said Terry. 'Last thing we need is a bomb dropping on the zoo and two hundred cobras and things being set loose.'

Joe stopped eating, lost in that thought, as if the image were playing inside his head.

'What's your name?' I asked.

'Doug,' and introductions were done.

'And how dae you know all this?' asked Joe.

'Oh, I spoke to one of the keepers. A few of them are still around.'

'Well, see if you can find out what the animals are eating,' said Joe. 'Because if I find out there's something in there getting the steak I've been denied then I'm gonnae go in there with a big knife and some firewood.'

'Did you know?' said Doug. 'They did that in Paris during the Siege in 1870. They were starving so they went through the zoo and slaughtered everything.'

'Like what?' I said.

'Everything. The most famous were the elephants.'

'I'd love to see that on a menu,' said Terry. 'Elephant and chips twice and a pot of tea.'

'So did they share it around?' asked Joe.

'I wouldn't have thought so,' said Doug. 'Apparently the best restaurants made up menus, things like 'Côtelettes de chien aux petits pois'.'

'What's that?' said Terry.

'Dog chops with peas.'

Laughter.

'I wonder what giraffe tastes like,' I said.

'Chicken,' said Terry.

'So it was the toffs that scoffed the zoo?' persisted Joe.

'I think so,' said Doug.

'And what did the workers eat?'

'Whatever they could I would've thought. Rats. Nothing. Many died.'

'Rats? Typical, isn't it? Even in France, the working man does all the work and gets none of the rewards.'

'How would you have done it?' I said. 'Even with two elephants there wouldn't be much to go round if you share it equally.'

'Put together with everything else, the rats, the dogs, there would be enough. There was obviously enough tae go round or everybody would've died. Take the rough with the smooth. A bit of nice meat and a bit of rat. Instead of the rich getting the choice cuts and the poor getting all the crap. Share it out and everyone gets the same treatment and everyone gets the same chance tae survive.'

'It's not really fair on the restaurants though, is it?' said Terry.

'How?'

'Well, since the restaurants are the ones selling it, I'm assuming they were the ones who organised it all, got the animals, slaughtered them, cooked and served the meat. And it can't be easy, can it? Butchering an elephant. That kind of entrepreneurial spirit shouldn't go unrewarded. I mean, while people were dying because they had no food, some clever soul obviously thought "hang on, there's a zoo full of animals, why don't we eat those." Now if you just give it away, what reward does the clever soul get?'

'Keeping his fellow man alive,' said Joe.

'Not a very good reward that, is it? I mean, okay you get a nice warm glow for a few minutes, but you can't put that in a bank, can you?'

'You think money is more important than your fellow man?' said Joe.

'Not necessarily, but one thing I know is that I can't hang around hoping my fellow man is going to get round to helping me, so I'm going to go out and help myself in the meantime.'

'That's how they win,' said Joe. 'Money is a tool tae better society, no a tool tae better only yourself.'

'Well, I've got to start somewhere,' said Terry.

'You bourgeois—'

'Hey, Jock, don't start that with me. I come from a family of miners, all of us were involved in the strikes, trade unionists to a man, but so far it's got us nowhere. Now if you want to go the Soviet route then fine, good on you, a lot of my friends feel the same, but—'

'Hadn't we better get going?' I said.

'What?'

'It's nearly one. We've got to get back.'

We finished up. As we were leaving the mess, Joe could hold it in no longer.

'Listen, first thing's first, if you ever call me "Jock" again, I'll—'

'Attention!'

We stopped dead, the training kicking in.

'What do you two think you are doing?' It was Hawkins. He'd been waiting just outside the mess. He was talking to Joe and Terry.

'Sir?'

'I said, what do you two think you're doing?'

'We're returning as ordered, sir.'

'Like that?'

I realised what he was referring to and was glad I'd done it without thinking. Terry and Joe both had their forage caps in their hands. Doug and I were wearing ours. 'You two, off you go,' Hawkins said. 'You two, come with me.'

Doug and I marched quick time, making sure we didn't break any of the regulations we'd only just begun to memorise. Joe and Terry would get a punishment drill. Joe was already beginning to rack them up.

It was non-stop. We took to testing each other, reviewing together, sharing out the pressure, the knowledge. We had a swimming test. Growing up next to the slow moving river Don, I'd had plenty of practice, but many couldn't manage more than a splash. We were separated, and the doggy-paddlers thrown in the deep end. While Terry and Joe were doing impressions of the Bismarck, we got survival training. Since Britain is an island, any offensive sortie involved crossing water. The chances of a dip in the North Sea or the Channel were high, and we had to know what to do when our kite crashed into the water with us still onboard. This was replicated by jumping off the top diving board beside an upturned bomber dingy, righting the dingy and getting in. In the dark. Fully clothed.

Instructors took every opportunity to scare the crap

out of us. Stories of crashes in sea, on land or in air, being shot down, captured, having legs blown off, arms blown off, being blinded, deafened. By the end of one lecture I thought that, when it came down to it, I might be better off dying outright than surviving as a cripple behind enemy lines. Dreams of floundering in the North Sea, burning in wreckage, riddled with ack ack. 'I tell you,' said Terry that night. We were on the roof doing our stint of fire watching. 'After this, being captured is going to seem like a holiday.'

'I don't think the Gestapo's idea of torture is to push you in a swimming pool,' I said. 'They don't want to know about wind flow over curved surfaces.'

'I just mean,' said Terry, rubbing his aching legs, 'that the Gestapo are bound by the Geneva Conventions. This lot aren't, not when it comes to how they treat us.'

The next evening was free. I dozed a bit, read the newspaper. Sfax, some Tunisian port, had fallen. The North Africa campaign was going well. I wondered where Willie was. His regiment had gone to Africa. I got a letter or two from him but they were so heavily censored all I could tell was he had pencil and paper. There'd been nothing since Christmas. Terry disappeared with his black market goods, God knows where, leaving me at a loose end. When Joe invited me out for a pint, I couldn't think of an excuse fast enough. He'd found a pub to his liking. Our first weekend was approaching, and we'd have some time to ourselves. None of us could wait. Time to consolidate, review, sleep. I needed time off. I was planning to visit the record shop in Soho, try and find out about any gigs. I'd asked a few of the lads around Abbey Road and in our flight, but none of them really cared much about music. Joe returned with a round, sat back down. 'What are you going to do this weekend?' I asked him.

'Are you kidding?' he said. 'Saturday night in London? I'm gonnae find a boozer, find a wench.'

Find a fight? 'Aye? Where about?' Make sure I'm not in the same area.

'Dunno. You any ideas? I'd ask the cockneys but they're no talking tae me.'

'No, I've no ideas. Sleep would be nice. A lie in. Go over everything we've learned this week.'

'You're gonnae use your weekend tae study?'

Joe never complained about the training, about being tired. Maybe he really didn't mind it, but Terry reckoned it was a Communist thing: he couldn't be seen complaining about a little hard work. I didn't really understand what a Communist was. What was the point? Politics was in London and no-one in the north could do anything about that, especially out on the farms. The only political person I'd encountered was Duncan Collins, who had gone to prison as a conscientious objector. I didn't really know him myself, but Dod had been one of the group who gave Duncan a real kicking outside The Clansman just after war was declared. It seemed to me back then that if political beliefs could leave you with a buckled nose and a permanent limp, they were probably worth avoiding. Joe himself looked like he'd handed out a few kickings in his time and maybe taken a fair share. 'So you up for it?' Joe said.

'Up for it?'

'The weekend. Out on the randan, lads' night out.'

'Could do.' Non-committal. 'But not a big night. We've got church first thing Sunday for a start.'

'Church? The fuck are you on about?'

'Compulsory church parade, Sunday morning.'

'No way am I going tae that.'

'It's compulsory,' I said.

'Aye, well, we'll fucking see about that.'

'Don't you go to church?' I asked him.

'Course no. Don't tell me you do?'

'We went sometimes, like at Christmas and Easter, but there's always work to do on a farm. You can't take a day of rest when the cows need milked or the field needs ploughed or the harvest taken in. Ma and Lizzie used to go. Lizzie hated it.'

'And you believe that shite?'

'I suppose so,' I said. 'To be honest, I don't think I've ever thought about it.'

'I had tae go when I was wee,' said Joe. 'Ma made us, Alec and me. Da didnae give a flying one, but Ma made us go. Christ, I hated it. All that gold and nice clothes and the collection plate. I couldnae ever work out how we had tae give money for the poor of the area when we *were* the poor of the area. We'd put some coins in like Ma'd told us cause if we didnae the Priest would tell her, and then we'd get no lunch. Then when Alec was about ten we just stopped going. We'd take the collection money Ma'd given us and go get a pie, something like that. Best meal of the week, that one.'

'Didn't you get caught?'

'Aye, but by then Ma had too much tae worry about with Da's drinking, and Alec was old enough tae gie her a mouthful. She still tried tae make us go, but she knew she couldnae force it. Then we started hanging around the Party, earning a bit running errands for them. They always seemed to make more sense than the church. They were all for helping the poor, no taking their money and using it for gold candlesticks and fancy dresses.'

Saturday after parade we were given our freedom. St John's

Wood was stuffed with RAF and we wanted to get away. Terry and I decided to walk into town. About halfway down Edgware Road, Joe caught us up. None of us had been into the city before, other than passing through on the day we arrived.

'So, what's everyone up to the day?' said Joe.

'A bit of business,' said Terry. 'Then a pint. Then I've a surprise for you, Jack.'

'What is it?'

'One you'll like.'

'I don't like surprises,' I said. 'Anyway, I've got plans of my own.'

'Oh aye,' said Joe. 'What you up tae?'

I waved my *Melody Maker*. 'There's a record shop in Soho.'

'A record shop? Did you bring your gramophone with you?' said Terry.

'No. But I just want to look. Maybe they'll know about any jazz clubs.' I'd slung my trumpet into my small kit bag, taken it along. I didn't want to be caught out if, by some lucky chance, some band leader happened to say *Hey, our trumpeter got bronchitis. Don't suppose there's anyone in the house who can stand in. Take a step.*

'Jazz? Now there's an idea,' said Joe.

'You like jazz as well?' I said.

'Course. I told you on the train, remember? Best jazz drummer in Scotland.'

'I just assumed that… wasn't—'

'You assumed I was full of shite?'

We turned left onto Oxford Street, busy, noisy. 'Well, you also told me you were a spy.'

'Aye, fair point. But no, the drumming bit's true. Mind if I tag along tae the club?'

'I don't even know if there is one, but aye, all right.'

'You said you were a trumpeter,' he said. 'On the train. Was that shite?'

'Nope,' said Terry. 'He's got his bugle with him. Stashed in amongst his kit.'

'Maybe he's hoping they'll make him the bugler.'

'The bugler?' said Terry. 'And do what? You think during an air battle they have a bugler in a kite buzzing round playing *charge* and *retreat*?'

We laughed at the image, a bugler in a Spitfire, canopy slid back, blowing away as we engaged the Luftwaffe.

'Right,' said Joe. 'I'm off tae Highgate Cemetery tae pay my respects.'

'Do you have family down here?' I asked.

'No exactly, but someone who's important tae my family. Karl Marx is buried there.'

'So, we get our first afternoon off since we arrived in this city and you want to spend it in a graveyard visiting a dead German?' said Terry.

'Aye, you got a problem with that?' Terry shrugged. 'Anyway, how about we all meet up in a pub later,' said Joe, 'and Jack can tell us where the club is.'

'Hey, what about my surprise?' said Terry.

'Can we no do both?' said Joe.

Terry thought for a minute. 'Sure, I don't see why not. Say, the pub nearest the Soho underground about fourish?'

'Aye.'

I nodded. What could happen at four in the afternoon?

'Right,' said Terry. 'See you later then, Joe.'

'Eh?'

'You're off to visit Herr Marx, yes?'

'Aye.'

'At Highgate Cemetery, yes?'

'Aye.'
'That's back the way we came.'
'Ach for fuck sake.'

The record shop was bombed out. Some time ago, it seemed. Half the street had gone with it. I went into a Lyon's for a cup of tea and a think. It wasn't even lunchtime yet. I'd the whole afternoon to myself in the capital. What to do? I looked through the *Melody Maker* but no inspiration. There were the parks. Sit on the grass with the paper, doze against a tree. Seemed a waste. My first weekend in London, to spend it doing what I'd do on the farm with a free half hour. The afternoon began to stretch out ahead of me. I was, I realised, looking forward to seeing Joe and Terry again. Both of them. They were an odd pair, Terry calculating behind an 'I-don't-give-a-fuck' facade. Joe all passion and energy. He probably did make a hell of a drummer.

I ordered another pot of tea, and started writing a letter home. I addressed it to all of them, though really I was writing to Lizzie. When I thought about Ma, jumpy, ever on the verge of tears, I couldn't think of anything worth saying. Da and I communicated in short bursts. A letter to him would be a line or two, and I'd be lucky to get a line or two back. 'You fine?' 'Aye. You?' 'Aye.' Lizzie was different though. She was seventeen, though I often forgot that she aged at the same rate as me. I had to count from her birth date to be sure. I wrote about Joe and Terry, described them to her, hoping she'd laugh. I told her about the London streets, the bomb craters, the people sleeping in Tube stations. Careful of the censors, I said little about our routine. I paid up, went back outside. Might as well take a walk, soak up the atmosphere. I retraced my steps to Hyde Park and went in. Getting off the road and onto the grass was bliss. Among all that concrete and stone, I was missing air breathed out by trees. I wandered aimlessly, drawn towards the water, the Serpentine, and toured its banks. On the other side I saw a uniform like mine, a face I recognised. It took me a moment but it was Doug, the lad from the mess who'd told us about the zoo in Paris. He saw me too and waved, pointed to the bridge. 'Afternoon,' he said. 'Having a stroll?'

'Like yourself,' I said. 'My plans were bombed out.' I was aware of my accent in front of Doug.

'A common hazard in London, I'm afraid.'

'Are you from London?'

'No, Yorkshire, but I've been down a few times before.'

'What are you up to today?'

'I was just on my way to the Natural History Museum. Have you been?'

'No, I didn't even know there was one.'

'Oh, it's magnificent. They have a diplodocus skeleton, the most awe-inspiring thing I've ever seen. Care to join me?'

The museum wasn't too far away. The diplodocus skeleton had been dismantled and stored in the basement but we happily passed a couple of hours with the fossils, marvelling not just at the array of extinct life that had walked the Earth, but at the people who had discovered a lost world. Random facts from school kept popping into my head, prompted by the displays. The science teacher at school, Old Milton, had filled my head with facts. A polymath the way all country school science teachers must be, he taught us everything from botany to thermodynamics. Most of it gone two minutes after the exams ended.

'I would've loved to be a palaeontologist,' Doug said. 'Like those Parish vicars, sermon on Sunday and letters to the Royal Society the rest of the week. Tramping over the countryside, digging into mountains to uncover the secrets of the planet, unearthing knowledge about the time before mankind ever set foot on her surface.'

'A nice career,' I said. 'Outside.'

He nodded. 'To piece together the deep past. It's almost impossible to picture what it was like when the dinosaurs ruled and man was a small mammal yet to evolve very far. Today everywhere you look there are signs of our presence. Even in the remotest parts there are the marks of habitation. Walls, ruins, scars of agriculture, geometric shapes, straight lines that nature herself would never produce. Back then, during the Jurassic, the Cretaceous periods there was nothing anywhere that was unnatural. Forests, jungles, swamps, deserts, mountains and seas, all of it teeming with life evolving unhindered by hunters, by logging, by mining or fishing.'

I wasn't sure if he was talking to me directly. Maybe if he'd been alone, he'd still have voiced these thoughts. I allowed myself to drift with his accent. I imagined Inverayne without any signs of human life. The dykes gone, the animals roaming free, no smoke in the air, no sound of industry. It did seem peaceful, but empty. 'The world would get on fine without us.'

'It would. The dinosaurs ruled the world once, and where are they now? In display cases. Stored in the basement. Who's to say it won't happen to us? Our time here is infinitesimally small in the span of geological time yet we fill it with such importance, as if while the dinosaurs were here the world was just waiting, killing time until we showed up to dredge the oceans, strip the forests and empty the ground.'

'So was that your plan before the war? Science?'

'I didn't really have a plan. The same as you, I suspect. We've grown up with this war. But no, as much as I love science, I have no real aptitude for it. Poetry is more my thing. Science can be beautiful but poetry always seemed more... perfect, somehow. More... deep. Deeper. Evolution is an elegant theory, but it can't fire the soul they way Eliot can. Have you ever read Eliot?'

'No.'

'So what's your passion?' Doug asked.

'Music,' I said. 'Jazz.'

'Ah, jazz. Listening or playing?'

'Both. I play trumpet.'

'Like Louis Armstrong.'

'You know Armstrong?'

'I assume you are a fan?'

'Satchmo? God, when I first heard that sound I didn't even know what was making it. It was unearthly. When I found out it was a trumpet I couldn't believe it. I'd seen a brass band play in Aberdeen one time, military marches it was, rubbish, and I couldn't believe it was the same instrument. Well, obviously we couldn't afford a trumpet so I got a wee pipe, and then a recorder, had to make do with those, but when I was fifteen my older brother, Dod, got hold of a trumpet for me. One of this pals at school had one but never used it. They joined up together, him and Dod. Do you like jazz, too?' I asked him.

'My brother is the big fan,' he said. 'He spent time in Paris before the war.'

'Paris? Nice.' The clubs, the smoke, the music. Clubs. A sudden thought. 'Do you know what time it is?'

We looked around for a church. 'There,' he said. 'Three thirty.'

'Damn, I'm supposed to meet friends at four.'

'Near?'

'Soho. A pub.'

'That way,' he pointed. 'But you'd better hurry if you don't want to be late.'

'Would you like to come along?'

Doug thought for a moment. 'Yes, why not? All I have to do is go back to the flat and the chaps I share with are not the most congenial of men.'

They were waiting. Joe gave me an earful. He'd already got a few drinks in him and herded us towards the bar with orders to 'catch up'. Terry was at the bar, chatting up the landlady or cooking up some deal. We got pints in and joined Joe at the table. He fixed Doug with a boozy glare.

'I've seen you afore.'

'Yes. We spoke in the mess.'

'Ats right. Elephant man. Dog chops.'

Satisfied, Joe lifted my pint and took a big gulp. 'Thanks, big man.' I rolled my eyes and got another. Joe drummed on the table, softly at first but quickly getting carried away. Doug lifted the glasses before they spilled. 'Get yer ain,' said Joe, taking both pints off him.

'You're a drummer then?' Doug said.

'Aye. Well spotted. Best jazz drummer in Glasgow, all of Scotland, everywhere, the world. You a jazzman elephantman?'

'No,' Doug replied.

Joe stopped drumming, fixed him with his glare again. 'No? What's wrong with you? Don't you like music?'

'I like music fine. I just don't play jazz.'

'What do you play? Accordion?'

'Rugby.'

Joe shook his head. 'Poor man. You should play something. Guitar maybe. You'd suit a guitar. Here, have a pint on me,' he said and handed Doug his own pint back.

'Where's that Welsh git?'

'At the bar,' I said.

'Good man.'

I was watching Terry. He'd finished talking to the landlady and had spotted a piano against the back wall, wandered over to it. I followed. He lifted the lid and fingered a few keys. It was slightly out of tune and the high notes tinkled more like cowbells than milk bottles but in a war you do what you can. 'I didn't know you could play,' I said.

He looked over at the landlady. 'Don't mind, do you, love?'

'Depends on how good you are. If you're a trial to listen to that lid's coming down on your fingers faster than you can say Duke Ellington. Is he with you?' she nodded at Joe.

'Sort of,' said Terry, sitting down at the keyboard.

'Well can you control the language on it? Never heard swearing like it.'

'We haven't had any luck so far,' said Terry. 'He's a Jock, you see. Likes his swearing. Something about a lack of vitamins.'

She went off muttering. He began slowly, picking his way through the first few bars, the tune rolling out. An upbeat number, swinging, but with a melancholy refrain. Beautiful. The piece settled into a three chord progression, bashed out, all complexity gone in a final climax. Repetition, and lots of it, but with an exotic hint of something. That's where the trumpet would be. I had it in my bag. Should I?

A few people clapped when he finished. The barmaid nodded; he could keep his fingers for the time being. 'Hey Taffy,' shouted a cockney voice. 'Enough of that darkie music. Don't you know any proper tunes?'

Terry rolled his eyes at me, then broke into *White Cliffs of Dover*, flattening every third note. The effect was nauseating.

A few still attempted to sing but that kind of treatment, the expert destruction of a melody as only a talented player can manage, carried all before it. The shouting quickly drowned him out. He moved into *Stardust*.

'Terry,' I said.

He looked up but didn't stop playing.

'You play jazz?'

He nodded.

'How come you never said?'

'You never asked. Why, you got a request?'

'You know I can play the trumpet.'

'No, but if you hum the tune I'll pick it up.'

'Fucking hell,' I groaned.

'Oi,' said the landlady. 'Not you and all.'

'Sorry.'

'Hey, love, it's a bit down isn't it?' she said. 'Couldn't you play something more lively. It's not a funeral.' Terry nodded, ran down the octaves and started a roll at the bottom end, building to a crescendo, running up the keys. People were perking up. I knew what was coming. Part of me really wanted to play but I was nervous. A swig of the beer. Fuck it, I thought. Why not? I ran over, grabbed my trumpet. *Hot ginger and dynamite, there's nothing but that at night,* Terry sang, his hands bouncing over the keys. The party was back on. A hot wind through the bar, warming hearts and clearing heads. Keeping my back to the bar, no eye contact with anyone, I puckered up, put the trumpet to my lips and blew. *They kissy and huggy nice, oh, by jingo, it's worth the price / Back in Nagasaki where the fellers chew tobbacy / and the women wiggy waggy woo.*

No improv, played it straight, counter-melody, syncopated.

'Fuck,' said Joe.

'Well said,' said Terry.

'I'm warning you,' said the landlady.

'What?' Was I that bad?

'That was fucking brilliant,' said Joe. 'How come you never said you were so good? Christ, if I could blow like that I'd tell the whole world. I'd walk around with the bloody thing jammed in my mouth.'

'Not a bad idea,' said Terry.

'You know what I think?' said Joe.

'You think Stalin should be Prime Minister?' said Terry.

'I do think that, but what I also think is we could have a jam. Drums, piano, trumpet. Taffy here can sing. Sounds like a band tae me.'

'Specifically, it sounds like a trio,' said Terry. 'But there are a few problems with that idea. One, we haven't got any instruments. Two, we haven't got any time. Three, I prefer to play solo.'

'Aye, heard that about you,' said Joe. 'Why don't you see if you can get us a drum kit through one of your "contacts".'

'A bar of chocolate is one thing,' said Terry. 'You think us business men walk around with drum kits under our coats? "Scuse me, sir. Want to buy a hi-hat? Shilling a snare?"'

'Well, thanks for your help,' said Joe, sarcastic.

I got another round in. We chatted about music, the latest gossip in the *Melody Maker*. A fight brewed over who was better, Tommy Dorsey or Benny Goodman. Obviously it was Dorsey, though his band hadn't been as good since Zeke Zarchy had taken his trumpet and left for Glenn Miller's band. Joe was having none of it.

'Hey,' Terry said. 'I promised you a surprise.'

'So you did.'

'It's almost time.'

'What is it?'

'Tits,' said Joe.

'Oi,' said the landlady.

'No, he's right,' said Terry. 'I heard tell there's a theatre nearby where for a small charge we can see artistic—'

'Tits.'

'—displays of women in their altogether.'

'The Windmill?' said Doug.

'Yes, do you know it?'

'My brother got thrown out of there for grabbing some—'

'Tits?'

'Yes, Joe.'

'Your brother sounds like a good man. Is he around?'

'Somewhere. He flies Lancasters.'

'Definitely a good man. Well, let's follow his example.'

'And fly Lancasters?'

'No, his love of—'

'Tits.'

'Right you lot, out.'

'Is this actually legal?' I said.

'Kind of,' said Terry.

'Kind of?'

'What happens,' said Doug as we bought our tickets, 'is that the girls reproduce scenes from famous paintings.'

'Nude paintings,' said Terry.

'Yes,' continued Doug. 'Nude paintings. Basically they recreate art and, as long as they don't move, it's legal.'

'So, they just sit there?'

'Or stand, or lie. It depends on the artwork.'

'And you can see… everything?'

'Well, again, it depends on the artwork.'

When we entered the theatre a comic was just finishing his routine. The bill was a rolling performance that started in the morning and ran late into the night. Because it was early there were still some seats near the front.

'At night it's usually full. Then you get to see the Windmill Steeplechase.'

'The what?' said Terry.

'When the girls' show ends and the people sitting in the front rows get up to leave, those sitting further back race over the seats to get as close as they can to the front before the next show begins. My brother's friend, Gideon, broke his nose trying it.'

It wasn't really what I'd been expecting. The place had a sunset atmosphere. Not many people want to have fun at that time of the day. I'd never thought that the first time I'd see a real woman in the nude would be in a theatre. Uncomfortable, like I was doing something wrong, shameful, hot under the collar. We sat and waited. I needed to think about something else. 'So your brother used to come here?' I asked Doug.

'Yes. Soho was his kind of place. Maybe it still is though I can't imagine the RAF let him down here much.'

'And is this the first time you've followed in his footsteps?' said Terry.

'The only time I've been here before was to take him home. We're not particularly similar, Edward and I. He wanted nothing more than to be a dilettante, to wander around Europe drinking, dancing, having affairs and breaking hearts. Unfortunately you need money for those kind of kicks, so apart from a couple of brief jaunts to the continent, Soho was as far as he got.'

'How come you're so different?'

'Different schools, different friends, different influences. I went to the local grammar, he went to a private school. I mixed with local boys whose parents could afford a bit of education but nothing flashy. He mixed with future civil servants and politicians. It went to his head.'

The lights dimmed and then rose. A woman lay on a bed, naked but for a bracelet and holding some flowers.

'What's she covering her fanny for?' said Joe.

'It's a Titian,' said Doug.

'No it's no, it's definitely a fanny.'

I didn't care what painting it was supposed to be. She was beautiful. Some of her long blonde hair was braided around her head, while ringlets ran over her shoulder, her breasts. I noticed a slight movement, enough to drag my attention to her face. She'd stifled a yawn. Even in the dim lighting, the look of boredom in her eyes was like cold rain. How many days a week did she work? How many hours a day? Standing rigid, one pose, then the next. After ten seconds the lights dimmed then rose again. Some scenes featured the same blonde from the Titian, others different solitary girls, some with groups of varying numbers. Doug kept up a running commentary of which painting they were representing. I couldn't help myself imagining backstage. These girls smoking, chatting, painting their nails, drinking tea. They were about my age, my year at school. Only a little older than Lizzie.

Minutes passed. To audible disappointment, the show ended. I stood but Terry gestured to me to remain seated. I felt vaguely sick. Did these girls come home and say 'Great news, I've got a job?' Did they pretend they were working in Lyon's Corner House? London really was something else. I imagined the outcry if a place like that opened in Inverayne. There'd be pitchforks and flaming torches before the first dawn, the Minister denouncing it as devilry. Who would go? The thought of Willie or any of the others ogling Lizzie from the front row. 'Are we ready?' said Terry.

It was still light when we got outside.

'Time for home,' I said.

'Time for home?' said Joe. 'Are you mad? That got me right in the mood. There must be a place around here somewhere.'

'There's a place that way,' said Terry.

'You're going to a brothel?' said Doug.

'Aye,' said Joe. 'Coming?'

'Not for me, thanks. With all the VD checks we're getting at the moment, it's not really worth the risk.'

'It's always worth the risk,' said Joe.

'Not for me.'

'Nor me,' I said, quickly. 'I forgot about the checks. We've got one tomorrow I think, don't we? I don't want to risk that.'

'You won't,' said Terry. 'I got you a sheath. You'll stay clean. Got to lose that cherry sometime.'

I didn't want my first time to be paid for in some backstreet with Joe and Terry outside the door shouting instructions. I started to walk away with Doug but Joe grabbed my arm. The force of it, the pressure right through to the bone. Doug left us to it. Soho was getting busier, the night approaching. GIs mostly, Army boys, Navy ratings, a few civilians. Joe was almost fully sober again and in need of a refill, but that was third in priority to finding the place and shouting abuse at the Yanks as they passed. Terry took us through main streets and side streets, into alleys and out the other side, he checked street names with locals. I was sure I recognised some streets. Terry described it as 'circling the target'. Thirty minutes passed and we were no closer. I began to relax. 'It should be here,' said Terry. 'Look. Crossroads here. Check. Post box on the corner. Check. Pub across the street. Check.'

'Where is it then?' said Joe.

'It should be here.'

'Well, it's no, is it? Some navigator you'll make.'

'Do you think it's where that building used to be?' I said, pointing at a bombed out gap.

'No, it should be a couple of doors up from that.'

'Well, it's no.'

For a few minutes Joe and Terry walked up and down the street checking each building for signs of life. Not much time left. The buildings looked like offices and it being the weekend, they were closed. But a brothel wouldn't have a sign. As they searched I leaned against a lamppost waiting, praying they wouldn't find it. 'You boys looking for the whorehouse?' said an American voice. I turned to find a GI standing there.

'Um… no, I mean… well, they are.'

'Gone, buddy, bombed out. Germans seem to have gone out of their way to hit it. Shame. Damn shame.'

'Shame. Yes. Thanks.'

'No problem.'

I went over to Terry and Joe and told them the news, trying to hide my relief. We had no choice but to head back to Abbey Road.

In some ways it would've been better if we'd found the place. The next morning Joe was angrier than I'd ever seen him. He called me a cunt three times before breakfast and nearly took a swing at Terry. And that was before Church Parade. He knew he couldn't skive. Hawkins was already onto him, and our next postings weren't based solely on exam results. As we walked through the doors Joe began muttering curses, chanting quietly all the hatreds in his heart. We were in our flight groups, so I didn't have to sit near him. 'What do you want to do after?' I asked Terry under cover of a hymn. We had the day to ourselves.

'I'm going back to bed,' he said. 'Got a week's worth of kip to catch up on and we're on firewatch tonight.'

He was right, the following week would be tougher. The first week had been broken up by medical checks and swimming tests. There was no more of that. It was study, study, study for the next two weeks, relieved only by marches. Back at Abbey Road, lying on our bunks, just the two of us.

'We could try and find a jazz club,' I said.

'Why don't you go with Joe?'

'Why don't we all go?'

'I'd really rather not.'

'Don't you like him?'

'I told you, he's trouble.'

'Only to people who refuse Scottish money.'

'Look,' Terry said, 'The politicos. Don't get too involved.'

'What do you mean?'

'I know guys like Joe. From back home. Lots of them down the pits. Communism isn't politics like being for Chamberlain or Churchill or whoever. Not to those guys. It's more like religion. Believers and Heathens. If you're not with him, you must be against him.'

'He's not that bad, surely?'

'I'm not saying don't be friends with him. I'm just saying, when it comes to politics, watch what you say, watch where you tread. You've seen it with all that Scottish v English nonsense. The safest thing is to do what I do and just not get into it with him. If I don't say anything, he can't get started.'

'You've met men like him before?'

'Back home. A lot of politics and a lot of coal dust. Sod all else.'

'It doesn't sound as if you like it.'

'Not much, no. Do you like where you're from?'

'I think so. Until I signed up I'd never been away from home, so I didn't have anything to compare it to.'

'And now?'

'I prefer it to London. London's too big, too noisy. No nature, no space.'

'You miss home?'

'Kind of. Haven't had much of a chance to think about it, to be honest. You?'

'Not even for a second. Best thing that every happened to me, this war. No way I'd have been able to get out otherwise.' He took a drink, shook his head. 'They really thought I'd follow them down the pit? Can't make a name for yourself in a village like that. You'll never be remembered there as anything other than your father's son, your brother's little brother. No, I had to get out.'

'What did you want to do? I mean, if there hadn't been a war?'

'London, this is the place for me. This is where the money is, and where there's money to be made is where I need to be. I understand the anger that drives Joe, you see, that bitterness at your lot in life. He wants to bring everyone down to his level, I'd much rather make it up to theirs. Live like the King. And you can't do that underground, covered in soot, coughing black, for the pittance they pay. No, there's money to be made in London.'

'With nylons and chocolates?'

'Yes, with those. Other things too. Whatever is there to be traded. Wherever there's demand, someone will step in to supply it.'

'Don't you worry about getting caught?'

'Not really. Only idiots get caught. Those not using their brains. That's not me. Although,' he laughed, 'it was getting a bit touch and go back home. Glad the letter came through when it did. The coppers were watching me. They'd turned a blind eye when I was young, clip round the ear and that was it. But eighteen is graduating, isn't it? Adults can't get away with what boys can get away with. It was definitely time to go.'

'What did your family say about you volunteering?' I said, thinking about Ma's reaction.

'Betrayal, they called it. Mining's a protected occupation, you see? If I'd gone down the pit I'd have been exempt from military service. So by volunteering I wasn't just giving two fingers up to the pits, I was giving two fingers up to the whole bloody lot of them. Well, fuck em. Betrayal? Fighting for my country? And it had to be the RAF of course. There's no way you'll catch me in some hole in the desert getting shot at by Krauts, Itis and Arabs. No chance. Do I look like a bloody fool?'

He dozed off, light snoring drifting across Sunday afternoon. I read the paper, dozed a bit myself, did some revision.

Monday morning, classroom, desk, teacher. The weekend over, forgotten. Head clear of everything but this. Everything from week one learnt, ready to soak up week two. The motivation made it easier. If we didn't pass there was no re-sit. We'd be washed-out and sent somewhere else. No Spitfires for us. Little banter now, the chat all about classes, checking points, clarifying things. Terry sat next to me in silence. I wanted to revise with him in the evenings, but he refused, he had plans. Business was good. Joe wanted to study with me, I could tell, but he'd never admit he needed help. He wasn't stupid, and for all his stories about never going to school, living on the streets with the Party, he'd passed the entrance exams. 'When I see a point in it,' he said, 'I can dae it. When I was fourteen there was no need for all that shite, so why bother?' He'd a good memory, and that had got him through the maths, but for what we were doing now, rote learning wasn't enough. You had to know what it meant in the real world. You had to be able to transform the letters, symbols and numbers into the flight of an aeroplane or the path of a bomb. Mid-way through week two, I hit on something that worked. I'd made the mistake of mentioning the beauty of algebra. Moving and realigning parts, turning the complex into the simple and back again. Joe didn't see it. 'Beauty in curves I get,' he pointed out, gesturing at the picture of a girl he'd cut from the paper and pinned above his bed. 'But turning those curves into equations is not going to give me a stiffy, you know what I'm saying?'

I tried not to know what he was saying and changed tack.

'You can read music, yes?'

'No,' said Joe. 'Never learned. Dinnae need it for the drums, dae you?'

'I suppose not. But you understand the concept of musical notation?'

'Aye, I'm no thick. I just never learned.'

'I didn't say you were thick. My point is, it's just the same as algebra. The black dots and lines on the paper aren't actually music. If you put your ear against the paper you can't hear Duke Ellington playing. They only represent the music. But if you can sight read, then as you read along the stave you hear the music in your head.'

'So if I had an equation for the curve of her tits and I put it into some magic machine that drew curves, then I could draw her tits?'

I wasn't sure about that, but it sounded right and if tits were what it took for Joe to pass the exams, then so be it. 'Yes.'

'And if I put that one into the machine,' he said tapping

my notes, 'it'd show me how a bomb falls through the air?'

'Exactly.'

'Why did no-one bother explaining it like that before?' Joe clapped me on the back. 'You're a damn good teacher, boy. See if you were on our side in the fight, you'd make one hell of a theorist.'

We worked through that day's notes, tested each other and both did well. I wanted to go over week one again, just to check, but Joe was done. Goal achieved, onto something else. He reached into his kit bag and pulled out a book. 'Here.'

'What's this?'

'*The Communist Manifesto.*'

'What's that?'

'It's the most important book ever written. It's the book that explains why all this,' he waved his hand at the expensive property we were sitting in, 'is built on slavery, on oppression of the working man. This flat is built on the blood and toil of men like us yet we're no even allowed tae use the front fucking door. It explains all this, and then explains what we can dae about it.'

I looked at it, wondering what it had to do with me.

'You're a bright lad, Jack, but your eyes are closed. You're no as lucky as me, you didn't grow up surrounded by the struggle. But that's no reason you can't learn now. Read this. But take care of it. I got it from my brother. Dinnae damage it or I'll damage you, right?'

'Right.' I'd never heard him mention a brother. I looked at the battered paperback and wondered what I could do to make it more damaged than it already was. It fell open at a page marked by a scrap of red material.

'What's this?'

'Gies that,' said Joe, snatching it.

'What is it?'

'Bit of the Red Flag. It was my brother's.' Carefully he refolded it and put it in his jacket pocket. I'd no interest in reading the Marx. I'd little enough time as it was. Apart from that afternoon in the pub, I hadn't been able to touch my trumpet, and with so much to read and learn, another book on top wasn't my idea of fun. I thanked him and put the book somewhere safe.

Marching.

Navigation.

Marching.

Maths.

Marching.

Air Force Law.

Marching.

We survived. Made it to Friday. One week until exams. Terry and I were crashed out on our bunks when Joe came in. 'All right, lads?'

'Knackered.'

'Seconded.'

'Great. Terry, you got?'

What was this?

'Yes,' Terry sighed, climbed down from his bunk and passed Joe something bottle-shaped in brown paper. Whisky.

'Dancer,' said Joe, handing over the cash.

'Very funny,' said Terry, handing it back. 'You agreed in advance.'

Joe looked like he was going to argue, bit his lip, took back the Scottish money and handed over English.

'You haven't been to change it yet?' I said.

'Course no.'

'He's been taking it off the other Scots,' said Terry.

Course he had. 'Right, lads, can I tempt you?'

I was going to revise but my head ached. I lay back, thought for a moment.

'Fuck it.'

Joe sat on the floor, Terry on the end of my bunk. The bottle cracked, passed around. 'So, anybody any ideas for the weekend?'

'How about some jazz?' said Terry.

'You serious?' I asked.

'Watching, not playing. I think I found a club, if you're still interested.'

'Fuck aye,' said Joe. 'And maybe another go at Soho. There must be somewhere I can get my nuts. It's been fucking ages.'

'Longer for this one,' said Terry. 'His is still in the packaging.'

'Fuck off,' I said. 'I'm not paying for it. Anyway. This club, Terry. You know where it is?'

'I think so.'

'Like the brothel.'

'That's right, blame me for the Luftwaffe's work.'

'So when are we going? Tonight? Tomorrow?'

'Tomorrow,' said Joe. 'I've got firewatch tonight.'

The whisky was half-finished. God help us if there was a raid tonight.

'Get the trumpet out, Jack,' Joe said. 'Give us a tune. You know any Louis Armstrong?'

I did.

The next night we set off early. I saw Doug at parade and invited him along. We spent the day studying, testing each other. Joe asked me about the book, I mumbled something non-committal. By dinner we were dying to get going. It was to be a big night: Baths and Brylcreem, uniform perfect, boots mirror-polished, forage caps placed just so. Our last weekend in London, it was going to be special.

We swaggered down the street, lads off out, stopping in random pubs for a quick snifter. Joe with a grin on him like a clown, Terry with nylons in his pockets in case his charm alone wasn't enough. A bounce in our step. Fags tapped against the packet. 'This is more like it,' Joe said. 'Never could wait for the evening fun tae begin. Alec and me'd get stuck intae a half-bottle before setting out. Some bravery juice for the birds. Swagger down Sauchiehall Street, intae every pub, or over tae the Barrowland for the dancing. I remember this one night. Perfect night it was. Half-bottle on the tram, pints in every bar. We're in this place near the Barrowland an Alec goes for a piss, when he comes back he lifts his pint and sinks it, then he lifts his whisky and sinks that. Only then we realise that he'd already finished his pint and never ordered a whisky. Turns out he'd pinched this massive fucker's drinks. *Sorry pal*, says Alec and headbutts him, Glasgow kiss right on the nose. Fucking blood everywhere and we ran for it, laughing all the way. We're more than half-cut by this time but Alec's pally with all the doormen at the Barrowland, Union connection, so we get in no problem. Alec's straight in about the birds, smooth as fuck that boy, had the looks and the chat. Well, that night he was straight in, nae bother, nae need for me so I wandered over tae the band, knew a few of them. Drummer was a pal and he wanted a crack at this bird he knew that was up from Ayr, so I sat in a few numbers. Then on the way home, what do we find? Mosley's boys marching along like they own the fucking place. Alec lobbed a pint glass like it was a grenade, straight in the headboy's face and we piled in.'

'No fighting tonight, Joe, right?' I said.

'How no?'

'We're in uniform now, remember?'

'Hey, it's never me that starts it.'

And we were there. Stone steps down to the basement, holes where the railings used to be, all gone for Spitfires. Didn't look much from street level: bins, a fire door, but down we went, past the bouncers in their suits, through into a red velvet lobby. A bored looking girl, our age, maybe less, chewing gum, took our money and waved us through the curtain. Terry pulled it back with a flourish, circus master, and I stepped through.

Deep lighting, lamps with red material draped over, candles in wine bottles, wax magma down the sides. The walls stripped back to the bare stone, modern artworks visible in the gloom. We moved between cabaret tables, swam through clouds of smoke. A woman billowed out of the gloaming and gestured at a table. We sat, ordered drinks, lit fags. Lost in the haze, oblivious to my companions. The stage empty. Sparkling drum kit reflecting candlelight. Upright piano side on, ashtray ready on top. Double bass resting in its stand. A number of other seats. The pictures in the *Melody Maker*, it was nothing like that. No orchestra set up, everyone in rows. None of that. This was something different. Our drinks arrived, we clinked. Drank deep. 'So what's the story?' said Joe. 'It's a house band?'

'Not too sure,' said Terry. 'A bloke I was talking to in another club said this was where musicians came to listen to jazz. It's unpaid so they can do what they want.'

'Grand,' said Joe.

'I figured if Jack was only going to get one chance, he might want to see something more interesting than Croydon's best Bing Crosby impersonator or a bunch of session players only in it for the money.'

I looked around the other tables. It was pretty empty but there were a few people, some Yanks in uniform, two couples, and us. 'It'll fill up later,' Doug said to me. 'No-one wants to be early.'

I was glad we were.

No dimming of the lights. No curtains. With no fanfare or announcement, five men climbed onto the stage. Piano, bass and drums joined by clarinet and tenor sax. Four of the five men were black, and three of that four in American uniforms. The drummer, the only white bloke, was a Royal Engineer and the fifth, the clarinettist, was Merchant Navy. The table of Yanks cheered loudly and we joined in. The drummer waved a bit, tightened his hi-hat. Drinks were placed in convenient places, fags and matches near at hand, seats positioned just right. No trumpeter, but no matter. Ivory tinkles, drum fills, cymbal crash, bars of something, scales, lips wet, fingers cracked. Nods, eye contact. Not a word but the music began in perfect synchronicity.

I was transfixed. The first note and the second note hard behind. No nerves on them, not that I could see. Not even looking at the audience, not even acknowledging us. The room could've been empty and they'd have still been doing exactly the same thing. How did they get that concentration, that focus? Blocking the world out and living in the music.

One of the two couples got up and started to dance. The Yanks looked like they wanted to dance too, but there was a distinct lack of women. Feet were going though, moving body and soul. I could feel it too, my heart beating with the soft brush strokes, the thump of the bass. Oaken rhythms, an unflappable foundation for the others to play off. And play they did. This wasn't Harry Parry or anything on the BBC. This was something different. At times I thought I could recognise a piece but it was never for long. The tempo was consistently high, each man improvising around the music, playing structures I couldn't quite work out. Oh, but it was good though. Not swing, not big band. I'd no name for it. Maybe it was the drink, crossing that barrier of intoxication, or maybe it was the influence of the music, but I was beginning to lose control of my limbs. My feet were dancing on their own, my shoulders shifting, fingers scatting over imaginary trumpet keys. I looked over at Joe, who was drumming an invisible kit. It was really swinging. Snatches of *Rum and Coca Cola*, bursts of *Body and Soul* at twice the speed. Extended jams. More drink arriving. Fags burning down. This was it, this was fucking *it*. I needed to be up there. *Tangerine*. They were cooking. The adrenaline, the sweat, the joy in creating and setting free. Each note in the chain something new.

A bang on the table broke my concentration. The club had filled up, the dance floor was full, uniforms everywhere, skirts spinning. The women had arrived. Terry was up dancing, close to a girl in a plain blue dress. Joe was dancing too, though I couldn't make out who with. His head was down and he reminded me of an Indian war dance from a western, something like that. Doug was watching me, I realised, smiling. 'I thought we'd lost you,' he said.

All I could do was nod.

At the back, the curtain shifted and a group of black Yanks came in. It made me notice that the only black faces in the room were on the stage. Odd. It was a jazz club, after all. Black music. The country was full of Americans, black and white. I shrugged, took another drink. There weren't any black people in Inverayne, but I wasn't in Inverayne any more. I turned back to the stage, turned my mind to receive. Time ticked, octaves and harmonics, I was out of body, inhabiting the music, ancient rites, shadows dancing, silhouetted by flame, embedded rhythms, rolls and dreams,

I left this world drawn in by clarinet, blown out by sax, flying, flying without a kite, without any need for maths and physics, navigation and weather charts, just twelve notes and no frontiers, the need to smash walls, break barriers, move into the new, expand, man. Whatever they call this it was mine now, it was in me.

I was lost, ideas and music, when a white Yank went through a table, Joe over him. Stunned, I spun, knocked my drink over. Another Yank took a swing at Joe who ducked, stepped, headbutted him clean on the nose then sank him with a knee to the balls. All hell broke loose. Fists and legs, glasses flying. The band cleared out, women screaming. Terry dived in, fists high. I tried to ignore it, stupid fear reaction. Step back? Leave? I saw another GI raise a pint mug, about to bring it down on Terry's head. I dived him, rugby tackle, and brought him to the ground. The GI swung at me, hit my ear, and I retaliated, catching him in the stomach, winding him. I felt hands on my shoulders and hands pushing me up, out. Dazed and my ear hurt like hell. Out on the street a voice said *run* and I did, down into the tube station and onto the platform. The voice was Doug's. 'What...' I panted. 'What's going on? What happened? Why did we run?'

'Police,' said Doug, also out of breath 'And MPs. We don't want to get caught brawling.'

'Terry and Joe...'

'They got out with us but they turned left. We turned right.'

The train came and we collapsed into the seats. I noticed blood on my hands. I pulled out my handkerchief and wiped it off. Not mine. Not cut. 'Christ, my ear hurts,' I said.

'No blood,' said Doug.

And I laughed, loud and hard. Everyone on the train looked at me like I was a lunatic. 'Sorry,' I said. 'What the hell happened?'

'I've no idea, I wasn't paying attention. I suppose we'll have to ask Joe. I assume he had a good reason.'

Home to our respective digs. Thanked Doug for looking out for me, went inside, washed off any traces of fighting, the blood and spilt beer. Terry still hadn't returned when I fell asleep, the adrenaline finally leaving my system.

Terry and Joe were there at parade next morning. How they got through without Hawkins or anyone else noticing the stink of alcohol or the uneven look in their eyes was beyond me. Sensibly, Joe kept his mouth shut as we were marched off to church. Back in our room at Abbey Road, Doug and I got the full story. It had started with the arrival of the black GIs.

'Aye, well they came in, got the drinks in, had a wee swig and then tried tae join in the dancing. Nothing wrong there, is there? Course no. So, one of them tries tae cut in on this Yank and the girl's fine with it, you know, she's just dancing, but the Yank clearly has a problem and gives the black Yank a shove and the black Yank tells him tae back off, so the white Yank's pals come over and give him some lip and so the other black Yank's come over and that's that, the first white Yank glasses the first black Yank so I get in there and gave him the Glasgow kiss and that's that.'

'I see you got involved as well,' said Terry, nodding at my ear.

'He stopped someone from glassing you,' said Doug, 'and got that as a souvenir.'

'Did you? I'll try and return the favour one day.'

'Joe,' said Doug. 'Do your nights out often end in fights?'

'Only the good ones.'

'Where did you lot get to? I thought you'd maybe got

arrested or something,' I said.

'No, we went out tae celebrate. If you two hadnae legged it the wrong way, we were gonnae take you along,' said Joe.

'The place we were looking for last time,' said Terry. 'It reopened in new premises. I'd planned a surprise. First gig, first leg over, but this one got you onto the train and that was that.'

'Aye,' said Joe. 'Your girl was very let down. I had tae dae her just to cheer her up. By Christ, you missed out. That was a night all right.'

'Two fights,' said Terry.

'Two?' I said. 'You didn't?'

'Joe tried to pay the girls with Scottish notes,' said Terry.

Heads down. Books open. Eyes front. Sunday to Wednesday we studied every moment. Even while marching, I was reciting equations and regulations in time with the crump of boots. We couldn't have done any more but that didn't help against the nerves. The pressure building. This was it. Fuck up and you're gone. No pilot for you, best you can hope for is a seat at the back of a Lancaster, having you arse shot at over Europe. No-one slept much the night before the exams, and I was glad I'd pulled firewatch. Reciting equations and laws to the searchlights and barrage balloons was better than lying staring at the bottom of Terry's bunk. If I'd been at home, out in the field with my trumpet, just me and the beasts, I'd have been blowing the dust away. Breakfast: Fags, and lots of them.

Differential equations.

Chewed fingernails.

Subsection 1, paragraph 3.

Fags.

Atmospheric pressure decreasing steadily, wind speeds

rising. Discussed an answer. Compared. Contrasted. Panicked.

Then it was done. Over the finish line. No celebration, back to bed. Route marches were a piece of piss compared to that. Our three weeks were up. We'd been drilled and marched and tested and lectured and paraded. The four of us passed. We made it. Joe gave me a pat on the back. On the final morning, at roll call, we were told our Initial Training Wing postings. Pilots, navigators or bombers – PNB – were split off from those destined to be air gunners or flight engineers. Joe, Doug, Terry and I were all classified PNB and were to be posted together to No. 1 ITW at Babbacombe near Torquay along with fifty or so others.

We packed, said goodbyes, trooped to the station, Hawkins watching us to the last, any excuse to delay us, repost us, fuck with us. We weren't stupid. Waited until the train was rolling, his sour face on the platform, and gave him the only salute a Sergeant like him deserved. Trousers down, arses against the glass. It was risky, he could call ahead and have us all on report, but we were done. Fuck you very much. London behind, one step closer to the sky.

'Holmes,' said Doug. 'You can't begin to compare Poirot with Holmes. Holmes solves real mysteries, overcomes dastardly criminal geniuses. Poirot is who you call in when a butler kills his master. Holmes is who you call in when the world needs saving.'

We were on the train from London to Torquay, lads squashed in every space. The four of us perched on our kit bags by the door, swaying like drunks on a ship, British Rail comfort. 'It's not exciting. Holmes is all sitting about fiddling, while Agatha Christie's books are page-turners. Holmes is an intellectual game, Christie is entertainment,' I said.

'What's wrong with using your intellect?' said Doug. 'You can work out Christie's plots by page ten. Holmes you have to follow and even after the last page you can sometimes only vaguely grasp the leaps of intuition and logic he's made. How can you not think that's more satisfying? I'd rather have a meal than a snack.'

'Using your intellect is fine but when I want to do that I'll read about navigation or something. When I read a novel

I want to be entertained.'

'Will you two shut the fuck up?' said Joe.

Terry nodded his agreement. 'No-one cares.'

'You started it,' said Doug.

'Me? I've never even read Sherlock fucking Holmes or Agatha fucking Christie. How could I have started it?'

'You brought up *Murder on the Orient Express.*'

'In passing. I was talking about something totally different. I didnae expect you two tae go off on a fucking what-dae-you-call-it, different path.'

'Tangent,' I said.

'Fucking tangent.'

'What were you talking about?' said Terry. 'Was it more interesting than this?'

'I was saying that if you were gonnae bump someone off, a train would be the perfect place tae dae it. Out the window or down the gap between the cars, body gone, no trace, by the time someone notices they're gone or someone finds the body beside the tracks, you're hundreds of miles away.'

'Cheery,' said Terry.

'Just saying.'

'I hope you're not thinking of anyone in particular,' said Doug.

'Don't worry,' laughed Terry. 'Joe's not a murderer.'

'What's that mean?' said Joe.

'Just that slipping something into someone's wine then dumping their body isn't really your style, is it? You're much more of a walk up and stick a knife in them kind of chap.'

'That would be one for Poirot,' said Doug. 'Although it would still probably take him all weekend. "Now here's the corpse and here's Joe standing over it with the bloody knife in his hand calling the deceased an f-ing c. I wonder what could've happened?"'

All laughed, even Joe. After a moment I said, 'Could you do that, Joe?'

'Dae what? Stab someone?'

'Aye. Well, kill someone.'

'He'd better,' said Terry. 'And you too. That's what we're on our way to learn.'

'No,' I said. 'I don't mean in a dogfight or dropping a bomb. I mean, you know, in a fight. Hand to hand.'

'No problem,' said Joe. 'Put a Fascist in front of me, I'll slash the fucker before he can draw breath.'

'How about you, Terry?' I asked.

'If it's him or me, then yes. I'd rather be the killer than the corpse.'

'No hesitation?'

'I'd hope not. I assume he wouldn't hesitate.'

'Hesitate and you're dead,' said Joe. 'Why you asking anyway? Of course we'd kill. All of us. That's why we signed up.'

'I don't think that's why we signed up,' said Doug.

'Well, they don't go for pacifism much in the forces,' said Terry. 'Sooner or later we're going to be responsible for someone's death.'

'That's not what I'm talking about,' I said. 'Of course in war you have to kill. And you're right, if it's me or a German pilot then he's going down. I'm talking about murder, not war.'

'What's the difference?' said Joe. 'If I shoot someone on Sauchiehall Street or in a Normandy village, it's the same thing. I pull the trigger, the gun goes bang, the other bloke snuffs it.'

'You mean in cold blood?' said Doug.

'War isnae cold blood.'

'I'm not talking about war,' I said.

'It's all war. Class war. Just because the Prime Minister didnae declare it on the wireless—'

'War is two armies fighting,' said Doug.

'War is two groups fighting,' said Joe. 'Dinnae tell me it's only armies fighting just now, because you try telling it tae the civilians in Poland, in Holland. Tell it tae people when the Gestapo bang on their door at three in the morning and shoot them against the wall.'

'So you could do that?' said Doug. 'You could knock on someone's door at three, line them up against the wall and shoot them?'

'I could,' said Joe. 'I'm no scared tae dae it. But then I'm more likely tae be the one against the wall.'

'How about in Russia?' said Terry. 'Stalin also knocks on people's doors at three and lines them up against the wall. If you were in your Communist Utopia, and Stalin ordered it, would you do it?'

'Stalin doesnae dae that,' said Joe.

'What about the purges, the trials?'

'They were enemies of the Revolution, enemies of Socialism. Every country executes people for treason. Happens in Britain just as much as in the Soviet Union.'

'So, if a court decided that someone was an enemy of the state and sentenced them to death, you'd carry it out?'

'Cannae make a better world without breaking a few eggs.'

'They're not eggs,' said Doug. 'They're skulls.'

'So the revolution in Britain,' I said. 'If it happens, will be violent?'

'It's no a revolution if it isnae violent,' said Joe.

'Like in France?' said Doug. 'Guillotines in Trafalgar Square? The Mall stained red with blood? The Thames clogged with body parts?'

'I need to get off this train,' said Terry.

Babbacombe, Devon. April – July 1943

Babbacombe was a beautiful English seaside town over-
looking the Channel. A crescent of sandy beach surrounded
on three sides by tree-covered cliffs, rows of pastel houses
and hotels stretching along the south coast. The English
Riviera, but rather than holidaying families, the hotels were
full of RAF cadets and officers. Spring was turning into
summer, with clear, deep blue skies.

Stage two. Fifty of us posted to Babbacombe, overlapping
with four other groups. In the evenings we were free to
lounge on the beach, easing tired bones. The sea was full
of men swimming, floating, larking about. It was hard to
believe there was a war on, that the Nazis were only a short
distance away. I came down by myself, leaving Joe, Terry
and Doug at the hotel we were billeted in. The beach was
busy, lads I recognised, new faces I'd met as training groups
cycled, pairs, threes, PT, Morse code, navigation. Some I
knew from London. Clive, Micky, Nev, Paddy. I stripped
and dove into the water, stayed down pulling hard against
the incoming current, feeling the rage of my lungs, finally
surfaced nearer the shore than I'd imagined, gasped in

air then set off, arm over arm, out towards France. Since arriving this had become the part of the day I looked forward to, rinsing off the classroom, stretching my muscles. There was a line, a frontier where the sea stopped being costal and became Channel. I could feel myself passing it, some geological border far below, the bottom dropping away and with it the temperature. Far enough. I bobbed for a moment, wondering if I could keep going, make it to France, see Jerry for myself. Contact. Then back, slower this time, breast stroke, inshore warmth, the noises of the lads reaching me, calling me in. Clive was up on Nev's shoulders, Paddy on Micky's, wrestling, first couple to fall loses. As I swam past I grabbed Nev's shorts and yanked them down. He mock screamed, threw Clive back into the waves.

'Good man, Jack, nicely ahhhh!' called Paddy, as Micky tipped him into the drink as well. A play fight began, five of us splashing, trying to sink the others, more joined in, the sea bubbling and frothing as 'U-boats' downed trunks, flicked periscopes, charged depths. Up on the road, locals watched us, some of them women, and that set us off again, headstands, handstands, cartwheels. I waded ashore to my clothes, lit a fag. Joe, Terry and Doug joined me, the four of us on the shoreline, the incoming tide breaking gently.

'Ah, a seaside holiday,' I said, lying back.

'You call this a holiday?' said Terry, massaging his aching legs. 'Half an hour at night to ourselves and the rest of the time square-bashing, running from hut to hut, cramming navigation, law, Morse code into our heads?'

'Mine's gonnae explode,' said Joe, flicking his fag end towards France. 'It cannae take it.'

'Mines are supposed to explode,' said Terry.

'No, that bit's not a holiday,' I said. 'Obviously. But I'm glad to be out of London.'

'So am I,' said Doug. 'The lack of horizon, the pollution, the people, the endless noise of people, the inability to ever be truly alone. It was like a hammer on my skull the whole time.'

'I miss Soho,' said Joe.

'I know what you mean,' I said to Doug. 'I felt it on the train coming west, like I was losing weight.'

'Hey,' said Joe. 'You reckon any of those animals from London Zoo are out this way? I mean, this is the countryside, isn't it? Maybe there's some elephants or something in a field.'

'Still,' said Terry. 'If this is a typical holiday in England, I'm not booking again next year.'

'I think they're trying to kill us,' said Joe.

'That's not very sporting,' said Terry. 'They should at least let the Germans have a chance.'

'See you, Jack, lads,' said Paddy, Nev and Micky on their way back. I saluted then gave them two fingers 'ENSA show tomorrow night,' I said. 'Anyone fancy going?'

The Entertainments National Service Association sometimes put on a concert in the little theatre.

'Every Night Something Awful?' said Terry. 'Not bloody likely.'

'You sure? They're looking for acts,' I hinted.

'You should've taken your trumpet down to the beach, Jack,' said Doug.

'The salt plays hell with it, took me ages to get it clean again after last time. The slides were caked in it.'

'Still, it would be nice to have some music.'

A human pyramid was being attempted. We watched in silence, willing them to succeed, willing them to fall. Down they came, screeches from the men, laughter from the road above.

'Idiots,' said Joe.

'You've always got to find time for a laugh,' said Terry. 'That's what we're fighting for, after all.'

'We're fighting so that everyone can fuck about?'

'In a way,' said Terry. 'Do you think they're doing this over there? No fun and games in the Third Reich.'

'So, just by sitting here, smoking and scratching my balls, I'm standing up tae Hitler?' said Joe.

'Yes,' said Terry. 'Symbolically.'

Joe flicked two fingers at France. 'I wish we could do something more than symbolic,' I said.

'Damn right,' said Joe. 'I want tae get stuck in.'

Letters from home asked when we'd be pilots, when we'd be fighting. Luckily censorship saved us from telling the truth. I don't think my folks would be too pleased to hear I was relaxing on the beach. I wondered where Willie was. Jerry had surrendered in North Africa. I hoped he was celebrating. 'Did I tell you ENSA are looking for acts?' I said.

'You did, yes,' said Terry. 'Twice in the last five minutes, once at lunch, and roughly five times every day since you found out. I'm wondering. Do you have a point?'

'Just, you know, drums, piano, trumpet. Why not?'

'We don't have drums, piano and trumpet,' said Terry. 'We have a trumpet.'

'He's got a point,' said Joe. 'I'm all for the idea of a band but best I can do is a wooden spoon and a dustbin.'

'So, if I could find drums and a piano, you'd be up for it?'

He thought for a moment. 'I'd be up for a session,' he said. 'I'm not committing to anything.'

'What's your problem?' said Joe.

'Nothing. Just don't see much point. We get a band together, play a few songs, do a turn at ENSA and then what? In a few months we're off somewhere else, maybe the same posting, maybe not. But if we pass here then it's flight school and the band will be over.'

'Fine, you're a misery, but if I find instruments you'll agree to try?'

'If it shuts you up.'

'Great. There's a piano and a drum kit in the hotel.'

'Our hotel?' said Joe.

'Yes. Mrs. Sutton told me. Before the war, before the hotel was taken over by the RAF, they had music in the evenings.'

'Well, Taffy?' said Joe.

'Cunning bastard,' said Terry. 'I'm in. But just this once.'

We set the instruments up in the corner of the dining room, empty after dinner. Joe sat at the kit fiddling with heights, angles. Terry ran up and down the keyboard testing the tuning. It wasn't perfect but not far off. I took out my trumpet, polished the bell. I blew a scale, ringing out bright. Good acoustics. Doug appeared with a tray of drinks from the bar, handed them round and sat at a table in the middle distance. Terry took a big drink, sat down at the piano and began playing a slow, mournful *Moonlight Sonata*. He was exceptionally good, eyes closed, fingers moving gracefully over the keys. 'Aye, all very fine and dandy,' said Joe. 'But we cannae jam tae the likes of Beethoven.'

'No, you can't,' said Terry, emphasising the 'you'. 'But maybe you can jam to this?' *Moonlight Serenade*. I took up my trumpet. The adrenaline. I remembered my first ceilidh and the thunder roll of the bodhran, the flighty buzz of the fiddle. But this was a real band.

Terry stopped, took a drink. 'Well?' Joe rolled out a rhythm, not too fast, not too slow, a platform to build from.

Terry came in with the bass, fleshing out the sound, then the high notes, a melody that danced around the familiar. I found the rhythm, focused on Joe's bass drum, took his syncopation as the springboard and jumped, tentative bursts at first, then finding my place between Terry's high and low hands, I began to weave a counter-melody, a counter-rhythm, slowly it turned into *Take The 'A' Train*. As that ended, without stopping, Joe ran a fill round the kit then slowed it right down, four-four slow dance rhythm. 'Show us what you got, Terry,' he called out. Terry hit the rhythm, straight into *You Go To My Head*, his voice clear and light, sitting snugly in the space left for it by his piano and me.

I stopped playing while Terry sang, coming in between verses. The voice on him. God, but he could sing. I stood back, listened and watched. It was exactly how I'd imagined it. The pieces slotting together, each note, each beat finding its complementary note waiting for it. I took a sip of bitter and dove right back into the music. We took a break when Joe demanded his next pint, and again twenty minutes later. How he could drink so fast while playing the drums was a mystery. He never seemed to miss a beat but the beer still disappeared. Doug sat listening, taking cash orders to the bar, tapping his feet and nodding along. He seemed to be enjoying himself. Terry made a suggestion.

'Shall we try something original? See how that goes?'

'A free jam, you mean?' I said. The idea. Playing blind.

'Not exactly free. I've got a few things I've written, we can use them as a base.' Terry stroked the piano, pulling a sweet soft melody from it. It made me think of green, spring, wind in the trees, a river. After a few bars I knew exactly where I would fit in. The piece was in danger of tipping into melancholy and needed a burst of sunshine. Should I wait?

Hesitantly, I blew a G, softly growing, like a dawn flooding the melody. Joe saw what I was doing, his head nodding. That was it. A D, F#, A the counter-melody opened out before me, tunnelling under the melody. Joe tanged the cymbal, brushed the snare like a summer shower, and we were all in it, all living the same scene, the same image in our minds. We were together then, the three of us, a trio in that moment. We made something that afternoon.

When we came out the hall, a few guys, Nev, Clive, Micky, and Paddy had gathered around the door. 'Was that you in there?' asked Paddy.

'Aye,' said Joe. 'How?'

'Yer cracking,' said Micky. 'You should be on at ENSA.'

'Told you,' I said to Terry.

'Being good enough for ENSA isn't a compliment,' said Terry.

'True,' said Micky, 'but play fur dancin, will you? The local girls won't have anything to do with us.'

'Music's not going to make them suddenly think you're anything other than a short arse,' said Clive.

We wandered through to the bar, revelling in the attention, rolling with the banter.

'You should play that new Nat King Cole number,' said Clive.

'Which one?'

'Nice idea,' said Micky. '*Straighten Up and Fly Right*. It'd be perfect for a RAF band. Signature tune.' Terry and I sat down one afternoon and worked it out.

Music we loved. Study we accepted as a means to an end. PT was a different kettle of monkeys. Running around with twenty-one other young men didn't in any way improve our chances of flying. It was simply the RAF's way of keeping us busy. Doug and I had no interest in competition with others. Terry's joy in sport came from gambling and even on the pitch he would be trying to run a book. Joe loved football, but his idea of tackling was to punch you in the balls. He was made referee: It was safer that way. We'd kicked around ideas for getting out of PT and making some rest and recreation time for ourselves, but none of the ideas were very good. Eventually though, Terry came up with something. We were walking from one hut to another, law class over and navigation about to start.

'Cross-country running? You've gone bonkers, mate,' said Joe.

'No, listen, it's genius.'

'It doesn't sound that great so far,' said Doug. 'Cross-country strolling, I'd be all for. Running, I'm not so sure about.'

'Daft. Pure daft,' said Joe.

'Of course we're not going to do any running, or at least we're only going to run until we're out of sight of the camp. The point is we use running as an excuse to get away for a few hours.'

We were listening. 'Instead of doing PT with the rest of them, we get permission to head off on a run and once we're out of sight we can go up into the cliffs where it's nice and secluded, have a game of cards.'

'Why not have a jam?' I said.

'Because I can't pretend to go for a run with a piano concealed about my person. If you want to try it with your trumpet shoved up your arse, I'm sure we can arrange it.'

'No a bad idea,' said Joe. 'Cards are much easier tae hide in a pair of shorts.'

'Well, you can take them then,' said Terry. 'No room for anything else in my shorts.'

It was agreed. 'Right,' he said. 'Bill told me about this

spot up the top of the cliff. Took this local lass up there. Says it's nice and sheltered, a little dip out of the wind. The game's poker. We play with matches, sort it out on payday. Right?'

'What about the wild animals?' said Joe.

'What?'

'From the zoo. We still don't know if there are any around here.'

Terry got permission from Evans, the PT instructor, and we found the spot easily enough. It was ideal. The Babbacombe Cross Country Poker School was under way. Every couple of days we set off for the cliffs, Evans encouraging us, calling on others to follow our example. They knew fine what we were up to. Some joined in, but never more than six at time. Terry held a raffle, at a price of course, for places.

Another day done, I trudged back to our hotel and found Joe sitting in the bar. He was at a table, alone, bent over a thick book. I joined him. 'Not still studying are you? I couldn't read another word today.' He lifted the tome to show me the spine and cover. Karl Marx. *Capital.* I'd never heard of it, though I recognised the name. The book Joe gave me in London. I hadn't even opened it.

'Marx again?' I said. 'Any good?'

He lowered the book. 'You didn't read the *Manifesto*, did you?'

I thought about lying, but decided it was too risky.

He shook his head. 'I've high hopes for you, Jack, but if you dinnae apply yourself, you'll amount tae nothing.'

'You sound like my mother,' I said.

'I was copying my own.'

I saw that Joe was still at chapter one. 'You just started it?

Or you rereading it?'

'Oh. Eh. Rereading, aye.'

'Looks like heavy going. Good on you for having the energy after a day like we've had.'

'You should read this sometime. All that crap the politicians come out with about trade and democracy and freedom is just bollocks. It's all in here.'

The bar was filling up, classes finishing, guard duty shifts ending. 'So what's in the *Manifesto*?'

'It's what we should do. This is why.'

'Is there a summary? I don't think I could read something that big, certainly not if there's no cowboys or Indians in it. Are there?'

'No. No cowboys. No Indians.'

'Ah. That's more my taste. You ever read *The Virginian*? Now that's a book. It's about—'

'Cowboys, aye, you said. Listen there's much more tae life than cowboys. That kind of shite is shovelled out by the state tae keep us down, keep us distracted. Same with the cinema. It's all about distracting you from thinking about what's actually happening around you. You see it every day. War's going badly? Dinnae worry, here's Henry the fucking Fifth.'

'Sounds a bit much.'

'Oh, it does, does it? You know they paid him to make that film? The government. Our taxes tae pay that posh poof tae prance around just tae distract us and tae make us want tae fight. Yet three years before, they were getting the newspapers tae print lies about what was happening in Spain tae stop people fighting.'

I put my hands up in protest. 'Sorry,' he said, taking a drink. 'Most people cannae even fucking see it. I try tae explain, tae teach people like my brother did, but I cannae dae it. Always get too tongue-tied, too angry. Alec, he always said I was a fighter, no a speaker. Now Alec? You'd have loved tae hear him speak. Must've been what hearing Lenin was like during the Revolution. Boy, could he get people moving, get the fire burning.'

'He's… I'm sorry, your brother's dead, isn't he?'

'Aye. Dead he is,' Joe quietened down, taking from his pocket the scrap of flag he'd had in the *Manifesto* when he gave it to me. 'Back in thirty-seven, martyred tae the cause, out in Spain.' The scrap of red flag lay in his hand, tender.

'I don't suppose you knew much about it on the farm? A real revolution. Alec said everywhere you went there were red Communist flags and red and black Anarchist flags. In some places they got rid of money and returned tae barter. You know, I'll give you twenty tatties for twenty carrots, that kind of thing.'

'We do that at home,' I said. 'Trade milk for bread, cheese for whisky.'

'Sounds good,' said Joe. 'Wouldnae work in Glasgow. All we had tae trade was our labour and once we'd built a ship, it wasnae ours anymore. If we owned the shipyard, the workers I mean, if we owned the means of production, when we'd finished building the ship, we'd own that and all.'

'How many tatties would you trade for the Queen Elizabeth?'

'The ship or the woman?'

'Either.'

We laughed.

'Is this in there?' I asked Joe. 'What you're talking about?'

'It's in the *Manifesto*,' he said. 'Gonnae read it, Jack?'

'Aye. Yes.' I said. 'I will, sorry.'

''Lo, Jack,' someone said. Nev and Clive. Nev went up to the bar, Clive stopped at the table.

'Hi, Clive, how are you?'

'Fine, fine. Just having a snifter before bed.' He saw Joe's book. 'Reading *Das Kapital*? Heavy going. Enjoying it?'

'Reading what?'

'*Das Kapital. Capital.* Sorry, I was using the German.'

'You've read it?' said Joe, disbelieving. 'I wouldnae have thought they'd teach this at your kind of school.'

'You're right, they don't. But I read it in my own time, just like you. Have you read it, Jack?'

'Nope,' I said. 'Joe's rereading it.'

Joe gave me a nasty look. 'Rereading it? Brave man. I assume you're a Communist then?'

'Course. I assume you're no.'

'No. I mean, I dabbled when I was more... immature, but there's a lot in Marx that is suspect, or just plain wrong.'

Joe leaned forward. I leaned back. 'Aye, well, you would say that. You're a rich cunt.'

'So? Engels was the son of a wealthy Capitalist. Are you saying rich people can't be Communists?'

I escaped to the bar to get a drink. It only took a bit of politics to ruin peace. Joe's voice rising.

'Course no. Daddy's built up a fortune exploiting the working class, you've got all the benefits but now you're gonnae pull the ladder out from under yourself, hand over the means of production and redistribute your wealth? My arse. You're just a toff playing at being a radical.'

'And you're not playing? I don't believe for a second you're rereading that. Don't get me wrong, I think it's great that someone from your background is trying to better himself, because surely that's the point of Socialism: background shouldn't matter. The Brotherhood of Man. Marx was from a well-off Jewish German family, Engels the son of a factory owner yet they could come together and write the *Communist Manifesto*. What my father does for a living shouldn't be held against me. Sins of the father and all that.'

Joe stood, fists clenched. 'Background does matter,' he hissed through clenched teeth. 'This is a class war. And you are no Engels.'

'And who are you? Trotsky?' Sneering. Joe lunged, knocked the table over, drinks everywhere. I was right to go to the bar. They'd have been all over me. But Clive was ready, side-stepped Joe who crashed into the table behind him. Joe got up, took a swing, right haymaker. Clive dodged him again, rabbit-punch to the side of the head as he went by. Joe hit the ground again. He got up, shattered bottom of his pint glass. Clive was faster, sucker punch to the nose. Joe went down. Didn't get up.

The MPs came in, carted them both off. We helped clean up the bar. Calm restored, I went back to the bar with Joe's book. God knew what would happen to Joe. Could be a punishment, could be reposted. Permanently grounded. I shook my head. Would that fight have started if he'd been reading *The Hound of the Baskervilles*? I sipped my bitter. Terry came in.

'Jack, there you are. Been looking around for you.'

'Why? Has something happened?'

'Has something happened? Only great news, that's all. You know St. Vincent's Hotel?'

'What about it?' I said.

'Requisitioned for military use.'

'So? So is the Foxland, the Palermo, the Devonshire, just about all the hotels in town are full of recruits and officers, including this one. What's all the fuss about?'

'St. Vincent's is different.'

'How?'

'It was requisitioned for WAAFs.'

'Aye. And?'

'A hotel, full, chock full of WAAF. Here in town.'

'That's good news for you.'

'For me? For all of us. I haven't forgotten your predicament, Jack.'

'I don't have a predicament.'

'Fine, but you'll come with us, yes?'

'Yes, why not? Just as long as there are no surprises.'

'Deal.'

I took another drink.

'Well?' he said. 'What are we waiting here for?'

'Now? No, not now. I'm knackered. Terry.'

'Fine, tomorrow then.'

'Tomorrow? I've got guard duty.'

'Right, the weekend then. Bitter, please,' he told the barman. 'So the weekend. Can't wait. Get Joe and Doug in as well. Where are they, anyway?'

'Doug's gone to bed. Joe's banged up.'

'Arrested? Politics?'

'Yes. He was reading Marx. Clive tried to start a conversation.'

'Idiot.'

'Clive? Or Joe?'

'So, Joe's still trying to read *Capital*? He's been at that since we all met. Don't let on I know, he'll go crazy, but he's been on the same page for at least two months now. Don't know why he bothers.'

'It's good to push yourself.'

'Not for politics.'

Joe and Clive spent a night locked up. Joe was raging when he came out. Humiliated to lose both an argument and a fight to a public schoolboy. I'd no problem with Clive, but I warned him to watch his back. Everyone knew Joe, knew what he was capable of. A dark alley, an ambush and Clive might not walk away.

It was my bet. I got a pair of tens, nothing else. Doug, ever gentle, bet two matches. Joe raised him five. Terry saw him. I folded. They might have been bluffing, but it was getting too expensive. I hadn't been lucky so far. Doug saw the bet, raised another two. Joe bet ten. Terry paused. He knew Joe was full of bollocks and would bet ten on nothing but couldn't be sure. He saw the bet. Doug shrugged and threw in the matches then, just as Joe moved his arm, chucked in another five. Joe hesitated briefly then saw him. Terry folded. Doug chucked in another five and absentmindedly scratched his ankle. His cards lay face down on the sand. He hadn't touched them since he checked them after the last exchange. Joe had his tight in his grasp, close to his chest lest anyone saw them. He stared hard at Doug. The wind picked up. His matches followed Doug's into the middle.

'Call,' he said. 'Two pairs,' said Doug.

Joe laughed loud, a harsh Glasgow cackle. Laid his cards on the sand. 'Full house. Threes and Jacks. Get that right roond ye.'

He started picking up matches. 'Hang on,' said Doug. 'I have two queens,' he placed the queens of hearts and diamonds, 'and two queens.' The spade fell next to the club.

We wanted to be face to face with Jerry. Well, we got our wish.

They came one evening while it was still light. They knew where we were. The evening, those off duty swimming, relaxing in the water, sleeping on the beach, a hard day over. Soapy's lot, Paddy and those boys at play. Jerry roaring in low, fast, no warning. Sudden burst of noise, the scream of planes shooting overhead, rounds fizzing up the water. The roar, the chatter. Rattle of bullets, bubbles. Soapy got it, riddled with the things, Micky, Nev, those two Geordies, couple of others. Out there, one minute they were letting the strain wash away, the next the Channel's turning red. Chaos, people going in every direction. Couldn't hide in the water, couldn't escape. Some ran for shore, some swam the opposite way. Others tried to go down hoping distance would be enough. It wasn't. You expect to die in war, but this was something else. Not combat. Some kind of circus. Jerry wasn't done. He went and let the cliffs have both barrels, unloaded into them, brought the whole lot down on the beach, right on top of Johnny, Davey, more, stretched out, lying down. Been asleep, woken by gunfire and next thing there's no next thing. Never had a chance. No way to fight a war. Shoot your opponent down in mid-air, best him in a dogfight, that's the way. Paddy and Ted appeared naked, covered in dirt and blood and there was this fracture, before and after, but you ran, ran with everyone else because you had to dig the others out from under that cliff, from the landslide, like it was some natural disaster, some act of God.

The anger around the place. Impotence was the problem. A pilot could get back up there and let Jerry have it, payback. Nothing we could do but wait. One day. One day there'd be a 109 in the crosshairs, a city through the bombsight. You vowed that, out loud, quietly to yourself, because nothing that bad should go unanswered. The voice at the back of your mind said it wasn't the worst that could happen, but that was just how you coped, it was how we all coped. You raised a glass. You cursed. You swore you wouldn't forget and then you tried to, because they'd be back and it might be you next time and you can't function

ng was easier than acres and acres of wheat. Doug didn't
mind either. He generally didn't mind anything as long as
he was outside. It was early summer on the South coast.
There were worse places to cut the grass. 'What would you
be doing if it wasn't for the war?' Doug asked me.

I paused, straightened up, wiped the sweat from my
forehead. 'This, pretty much.'

'Was the farm your future?'

'It wasn't. But then Dod bought it.'

'Your brother?'

'Aye, he was five years older than me. In it from the start.
Dunkirk.'

'There was just the two of you?'

'A sister as well. Lizzie.'

'So you're the man now.'

'I'm the man, now. If I survive all this, I'll have to take
over the farm.'

'How do you feel about that?'

'No choice. No point in feeling anything about it.'

'If your brother hadn't... what would you have done?'

'You know what? I really don't know. By the time it
started to become real, it was '39 and the war was on. Since
then there hasn't seemed much point in planning. And then
Dod died and that was that.'

'No point planning,' Doug said. 'That's a good way of
putting it. There's no point in mapping out a future when
you could be dead by Christmas. Not that it stopped me.'

'What did you want to do?'

'Cambridge. University. A future in the quads
surrounded by books and scholars. Maybe a thin poetry
collection.'

'Well, we might make it through. Someone has to.'

'Do you know Wilfred Owen? He was a poet who fought

with a thought like that slap bang centre in your life, so
it was nothing personal, nothing you wouldn't expect the
others to do when it was your turn. You pushed it aside and
you got on with things. We had to get our wings, get into the
game and then, and only then, when we pulled the trigger,
could we spare a thought for those two Geordies, Micky,
Nev, Dod and the others.

All the others.

The summer went on but no-one noticed. Heads down,
shoulders bent. The volume turned low. Letters home were
shorter. No news we wanted to talk about. No-one went
swimming any more. It didn't seem right to lark around
and though most wouldn't admit it, we were terrified. We
had a service. Silence. Salutes. More ghosts. Apologised to
them, promised they hadn't died in vain. The country was
haunted. After the funerals everyone censored themselves:
Not too loud, not too irreverent. Heads went into books
and stayed there. No jokes. Few conversations that weren't
directly about the business at hand. We played a bit but no-
one had a taste for it. Minor keys, low notes, slow tempos.
We were going to offer our talents to ENSA but now we held
back. In a world of ghosts we each retreated into ourselves.
I sat alone in a tea shop, staring at the pot. Homesick.
Thinking about those deaths. Thinking about Dod. Days.
Wake, study, eat, sleep. Nights. Distraction, anything.

Gradually we got back into playing, Joe taking his frustration
out on the kit. Straighten up and fly right. I told the ENSA
rep we existed, he promised an audition for the next show.
Whether we'd ever get there was debatable. Joe seemed
intent on causing trouble. He still wanted revenge on Clive,
but no opportunity presented itself. Clive wasn't daft. Then
he managed to get between Terry and a hotel full of WAAFs.

To practice Morse code we sat in separate huts and were given messages to send. They must've been extracts from poetry, some Shakespeare I recognised from school. If we'd been in the same hut, I could've asked Doug about the rest. All those *thous* and *thines*, we might as well be spelling out code as English, which was probably the point. Never send plain English, not in a war. The headaches it gave, the concentration. Felt like Glasgow-kissing brick walls, and that was just part of the day. That wasn't even the Air Force Law. Joe and I were in one hut, Terry and Doug in the other. We'd been at it for thirty minutes, thirty more to go, taking turns to send, receive, swap over. Receive a paragraph then send it back for verification. Chinese whispers in dots and dashes. If there was one letter out of place in the reply we'd have to start again. Repeat. Always repeat. Repetition was the watch word of the military. 'Message incoming,' said Joe, transcribing. "F – U – C – K – I – N – G – Q – U – E – E – R – J – O – C – K – S.' That Welsh bastard. Thinks he's funny, does he? Right.' Tapping. It was a long message but I could spot the repetition of certain letter combinations, F – U – C and K generally. I took a quick peek outside to make sure no-one was coming. If the Sergeant caught us, he'd rip our balls off for pissing around with RAF equipment on RAF time, pushing out his over-long neck to shout at us. Sergeant Cotters was nice enough, usually, but he had little time for anything out of line. We had to show our transcriptions to Cotters once the hour was up so he could check our progress. The reply came through. 'W – H – A – T – I – S – A – W – O – N – K – E – R – ?'

'Fuck,' said Joe. Sent his message again.

'Is this really a good idea?'

'Not letting that fuck get away with that. Keep a watch though.'

I watched. Suddenly from behind me:

'Bastard! Fucking Welsh cunting bastard!' J the door, belted across the parade ground. I turn the table and looked at the notepad. 'H – A – V – U – R – E – A – D – C – A – P – I – T – A – L – Y –

'Oh shit.' I considered briefly sending Terry a but Joe would be there by now. Anyway, Terry w have sent a firework like that and not then been looki the window. I went to the door. Beyond the hut I coul Joe chasing Terry between the buildings of the camp across the parade ground while Cotters stood shouting the pair of them, his neck arcing out from his rotund bod a look that earned him the nickname 'Turtle.' Most of u liked him, but a Sergeant was a Sergeant, and their job was to keep us in check. Why could Joe not control his temper? Why did Terry have to wind him up? I went back to the table and ripped the top page off the notebook, quickly rewrote the messages we had legitimately sent, shoved the incriminating paper into my pocket. A final check to make sure there was no evidence of mucking about and I walked slowly over to where the Turtle had finally got Joe and Terry to stop. Doug saw me from the other hut and did the same. I didn't know what Turtle would do, but I had a feeling we wouldn't have a free weekend.

I was right. Saturday and Sunday were taken up with menial tasks and extended periods of guard duty. Joe and Terry, as the main culprits, were cleaning the latrines, cleaning the trucks, cleaning the classrooms. Doug and I, complicit but not actually guilty of fighting and swearing in front of Turtle, were ordered to cut the grass throughout the camp. I didn't mind this so much: It reminded me of home, of harvest, but with the added benefit that grass an inch or two

in the First War. He died a week before Armistice. Yes, we might make it. But the war isn't the only reason I won't be going to Cambridge. You need money for that and we don't have any of that anymore. Too old for a scholarship. No, my chance disappeared when the mill went under. My brother, Edward, was the last in our family to enjoy the privilege of doing what he wanted.'

We lapsed into silence, thoughts on impossible futures, bodies getting on with the job at hand. 'I suppose I'll go home though,' Doug said at length. 'If I get through the war. It's only been a couple of months and already I'm getting homesick. What I'll do there is another thing. It will just be nice to get out of this uniform and back into some comfortable clothes. Do you get homesick?'

I thought about it. 'No, not really. I mean, I miss my folks, and a couple of pals, but since Dod died, and everyone disappeared into the forces, it's like the place became a ghost town. I was there for a year after signing up. It was empty.'

'A town of old people and women?'

'Yes.'

'It was the same for me. So, what would you do, if you had the option?'

'A job? The future? I don't know.'

I imagined I was on the farm, lost myself in the familiarity. Doug recited poetry to himself, body moving in poetic lines, work and words, movement and rhythm, the sounds of existence.

We strutted down the road, lions on the prowl, shoulders back, heads high. Just the four of us, Terry had made that clear. No competition. A military hardness to our walks that hadn't been there at the start of the year, but we weren't marching, we were hunting. Well, I wasn't, not the way Terry and Joe were, but for months now it had been nothing but the company of men. I wasn't on the pull – I'd have happily gone for a tea with Lizzie, just for a change of chat, a different perspective. Even Doug, who professed disinterest in the whole scheme, was caught up in the mood. We'd had a few drinks in the hotel bar, the warmth of it was enlivening. This was nothing like Soho. It wasn't far to the WAAF hotel. Terry took the lead, marching in through the door like a millionaire on the Riviera or an old boy arriving at his club. We followed him all casual steps, smoking. 'Oi, where do you lot think you're going?' The harsh military voice, the put on accent masking a working class one, the shrill tones meant only one thing: A Napoleon.

'Urgent secret business, sir,' said Terry.

'Not in 'ere you're not. This 'ere 'otel is reserved for WAAFs and while you may look like fairies, you certainly ain't no WAAFs. So clear off out of it.'

'Now, look here, sir,' said Terry, affecting a posh accent. 'This is an hotel is it not? And hotels have public bars, do they not? All my colleagues and I wish to do is enjoy our evening off with a beverage or two in this here fine establishment.'

We were attracting a small crowd in the lobby, all those pretty WAAFs in their uniforms, and it was making Terry brave. 'I've told you no. Now bloody 'op it. I know what you're after, the four of you, dirty little beggars.'

'If I may ask, sir, what you are doing here?'

'I'm 'ere to keep riff raff like you out. Now sod off before I have you on a charge for insubordination.'

'Now, look here, sir,' Terry tried again. 'I think it's dreadfully unfair that the men should be barred from entering a public bar while the officers are free to enjoy the, ahem, amenities of the locale. I mean, we're all in this war together, aren't we? What do you say, sir?' he said, dropping the accent, and his voice. 'Turn a blind eye for half an hour and let us have a crack at these lovely ladies?'

'Right,' he shouted. 'That's it, you four—'

'Ah Danny, there you are!' said an Irish voice, followed by a female body cutting between us and the officer. She grabbed Terry by the arm. 'Come along Danny, we're late enough as it is.'

Stunned though Terry was, he recovered quickly enough to join the charade. 'Ah there you are, my dear. I was just having a lovely chat with the Sergeant here.'

'Sergeant Dudley,' she said. 'This is my brother, we're going out for a while.'

'But Miss—'

'Sergeant, you know better than that. I'm First Officer Keane, not 'Miss' anything. You wouldn't like it if I called you Mr Dudley, so be kind enough to treat me the same. Now, we're late enough as it is, so if you'll excuse us.'

Not giving him space to respond she marched Terry outside, us three following behind and three girls after. When we got out of sight of the hotel, she stopped.

'That was very nice of you,' said Terry. 'I'm Terry.'

Her red hair was pulled tight under her cap but frizzy strands were bidding for freedom. 'That was a very stupid thing you did back there. Dudley is a nasty little man and would've had you breaking rocks for cheeking him like that. What did you think you were doing, anyway? Did you seriously think they'd let male cadets swan into a hotel full of women? They weren't born yesterday. Now, introductions. This is Mavis, Rose, Mary and I'm Winnie,' she said, indicating the three women who had caught up with us. 'You're Terry, and these are?'

'Joe.'

'Doug.'

'Jack.'

'Pleased to meet you all, we're sure. Now, let me guess,' she said, turning back to Terry. 'You were planning to get into the bar at the hotel, find some gullible sap, feed her strong drink then attempt to have your wicked way with her?'

'Aye,' said Joe.

I rolled my eyes. She spotted it, turned to me. 'Is that what you're after?' she challenged me. 'Are you after getting into our knickers?'

I blushed at the language, but I liked her, she reminded me of Lizzie, that spark, that force. When I was younger, the constant ribbing from Lizzie, her habit of turning everything into a dig at me, was infuriating. Now I realised I missed it. 'No,' I said. 'But the Queen's Head has got some Algerian wine in, and these three haven't got the sophistication for a drink like that.'

'And you think we have?'

'Are you saying you haven't?'

'What do you think girls? Wine?'

'Wine not?' said the tall brunette. We all groaned.

The pub was quiet when we entered. We got a couple of round tables near the back. Like us, the women were from all over the country. Winnie from Belfast, Mavis, the one who made the pun, from Surrey, Rose and Mary were both from Liverpool. I was beginning to learn about English accents, to divide them by geography, which ones were northern, which southern. Some of them still baffled me, though. I knew what a Geordie sounded like, but it didn't mean I could understand him. Liverpool I could manage, and Surrey was easy. Belfast was a new one on me, but it was more or less Scottish, so I was fine. The bar was quiet, just a couple of lads playing darts, an old local at the bar drowning himself. Terry and I got the drinks in, a tray each on the way back. The Algerian red was sharp, acidic. I wondered if Willie had drank this stuff, if he'd been in Algeria. I'd never drank wine before, but it was what they drank in Paris, in the jazz clubs. That and absinthe, but there was none of that in Babbacombe. Joe stuck to beer, the rest of us split a bottle. 'So, what are you WAAFs doing in Babbacombe then?' asked Doug.

'Oh, we're not WAAF. We're ATA. Air Transport Auxiliary,' said Winnie. 'We're pilots.'

'Pilots?' I said.

'Yes,' said Rose. 'We move planes around the country. Last week we took a fleet of new Lancasters straight off the production line out to well, shouldn't really say where.'

'You flew Lancasters?' said Joe, unbelieving.

'Of course,' said Winnie. 'How do you think they get from the factories to the airfields? You think they drive them along the road?'

'No, I thought it was proper pilots that did it.'

'Proper pilots, is it? And just what is a proper pilot? One with an extra stick in the cockpit, I'd guess. Well, let's see, hands up all those here who've ever flown a kite. No? Only us little ladies? Ever even been in one?'

'No, I'm just saying,' said Joe, digging himself further down, 'that when you think of pilots, you think of men, don't you?'

'Do you?'

'There you go, Joe,' said Terry. 'Maybe you should factor more women into your Socialist Utopia. You're going to need women like this in your People's Republic of Scotland.'

'You're a Red, then?' Winnie asked him.

'I am,' he said, proudly, jumping onto firmer ground.

'Don't puff yourself up there. You're in company. The

four of us are Comrades, too. And don't look so surprised. Don't tell me only men are allowed to have politics in Glasgow?'

'No, no, it's just—'

'You can't think yourself progressive and radical if you hold onto old-fashioned views. You really think when the revolution comes we're just going to sit quietly at home, knitting and cooking, and let you men make a complete mess of the world a second time over? Oh no, you lot have run it long enough, and look where it's got us. Well, now it's our turn. Listen, you must've heard of Ethel MacDonald?'

'Who's she?' I said.

'An anarchist from Glasgow,' said Joe. 'Went out tae Spain during the war. Aye, I know her. She was there the same time as my brother.'

'Your brother was in the International Brigade?' said Mary.

'He was, aye.'

'He died out there, didn't he,' said Mary. 'I'm sorry, it's just, so did my brother.'

'Aye, he did. In Brunete. How about your brother?'

'In Barcelona.'

They more or less split off from the group, sharing and comparing memories. I looked at Rose, trying to think of something to say.

'What's it like? Flying, I mean.'

'Nothing like it,' she said, and the others nodded. 'Up there, by yourself, that's freedom that is.'

I tried to imagine it. The closer we got to flight, the more real it became, the less I could actually picture it. At home, in my room, up in a tree, it was easy, swooping and diving. Here, weeks away? Blank. I realised I'd tuned out, the conversation had moved on. 'How come they always name these places after Kings and Queens?' Rose said. 'It's not like any of them ever set foot in anywhere like this. Why not name them after real people?'

'Kings are real people,' said Mavis. 'I mean, they're not imaginary.'

'You really think people would want to go to a pub called "Joe's Head"?' Terry said. 'Or "Jack's Nose"? "Doug's Ears"?'

'Henry the Fifth went to a lot of pubs,' said Doug. 'At least, he did before he was King. In Shakespeare's Henry IV part I—'

"Mary's Arse" said Winnie.

'No, it's true,' said Doug.

'No, "Mary's Arse" would be a good name for a pub.'

'I don't think so,' said Terry.

'Why? What's wrong with "Mary's Arse"?

Mary was quietly going beetroot in the corner.

'Nothing,' said Terry. 'But if you take a phrase like "I'm just going up The Queen's Arms," it doesn't work.'

'Oh, I don't know,' said Winnie. 'I think it has a nice ring to it. "Hey lads, fancy going up—"'

'WINNIE!' Mary shrieked.

Winnie cackled. Terry laughed. 'So, I assume you ladies aren't politically opposed to music?' he said.

'Not at all,' said Winnie. 'Why, are you going to ask me to dance?'

'I would if there were any music here,' he said. 'But the three of us are a trio, jazz. I was thinking you all might like to come and listen to us play sometime.'

'You play concerts? With ENSA?'

'Not yet, but we've got an audition tomorrow for the next show. Until then I thought you might like to come back and hear us.'

'Oh, back to your hotel is it? You're a fast one, aren't you?'

'Aye, that's an idea, Terry,' said Joe. 'Are you interested Mary?'

Doug and I looked at Mavis and Rose. They smiled, friendly but non-committal. 'Well, we'll think about it,' said Winnie. 'Although we'd much prefer a proper dance. Sitting watching you three sounds a little too much like a piano recital for my tastes. If you can get a dance organised, let us know. You can find us at the hotel. I'll tell Sergeant Dudley to keep an eye out for you.'

She stood. The other women followed her lead. 'You're not going, are you?' said Terry.

'We are,' said Winnie. 'Thanks for the drink. Let us know about that show.' With a final smile at Terry, she marched out the door. Mary bid Joe goodbye and the other two nodded at Doug and I. Crestfallen, back to our drab foursome, we settled in and got drunk.

Next day Evans, the PT instructor, was waiting for us. Something about his walk, the smile, an aura, something. This was going to be a problem. 'Hello boys, how's it coming?'

'All right, sir,' I said. 'Well, boys, I have some good news for you. Next week is the ITW sports day. We're competing against the other ITWs in the area and I've entered you all into the cross-country run.'

'You've done what?' said Joe.

'Well,' said Evans, 'you're the most enthusiastic athletes we have here, so I knew you'd jump at the chance. It's next Sunday, from oh-nine hundred hours. I'd suggest getting into training but I know I don't need to tell you boys that. Best of luck. You'll be representing Number One ITW.'

We all looked at Terry.

'Don't worry,' he said, pale. 'I'll think of something.'

'Aye, that'll be good,' said Joe. 'Just what we need. Another of your smart ideas. God, why dae I listen tae you?'

'We need a sick note,' I said.

'No chance,' said Terry. 'Not all four of us.'

'Well, what are we going to do?'

'I'll think of something.'

The audition was that evening. We set up and ran through our four-song set. We sounded all right, but nothing special, nothing to get excited about. I couldn't work out what was wrong – nerves maybe or lingering post-attack blues. We looked at each other, searching for an answer. 'I know,' said Terry, and left the hall. He returned a minute or so later with what must have been everyone in the bar. Bill, Pete, Chalky, most I didn't really know. Clive wasn't there. He avoided our bar these days. They settled themselves around the tables, their pint mugs out of place on the white tablecloths. 'Jazz in an empty room is like drinking a pint in your kitchen,' he said. 'It's better than nothing, but not how it should be done.'

An audience. Shit. 'From the top?' said Terry. I turned my back to the watchers. Focused on Terry and Joe. *Nagasaki* went well, and we got a round of applause at the end. My first. During the intro to *Tangerine*, I heard the squeak of the door, looked. Bryson, the ENSA rep, had arrived. I nodded at Terry. He knew. This was it. His left hand jumped higher, the bass bouncing along infected me, trumpet up, this was it, the moment it became serious. Not just pals having fun, a band, a real band and maybe, if we didn't fuck up, a real show. We finished our set with *Straighten Up and Fly Right,* got a cheer so big they must've been taking the piss. Doug took over drinks for us and the lads clinked glasses, patted us on the back. Bryson waited for the scrum to clear then came over.

'Not bad,' he said. 'I can give you four numbers near the start of the show this weekend.'

'Done,' I said.

The theatre was tiny. An old proscenium, ageing velvet curtains. Soft seats worn almost flat. Out front was more like a football match than a night at the theatre. Drinks had been drunk, and the merry saw no need in waiting for the show to start. Obscene versions of famous tunes rattled the cobwebs.

Backstage was pandemonium, a hurricane of lost props, half-complete costumes, AWOL cast. The three of us kept out of it, a bottle of whisky Terry had 'found' to warm ourselves. I needed as much liquid support as possible. I wished Lizzie was there, or Willie.

I'd heard the expression 'butterflies in the stomach' and thought it a poor description. Whatever was churning up my insides was a lot weightier than a butterfly. My stomach felt more like a sack full of chickens, like a sock full of frogs. I was going to throw up. I sat on the floor hoping the whisky would settle down the menagerie in my belly. 'All right, love?' said Doris, the woman in charge backstage. 'You look like your girl's just run off with a Yank.'

'You don't look too good,' said Doug.

'How did you get back here?' I asked him.

'I told them I was your manager. It's chaos, no-one's paying attention. Are you all right?'

'Bit nervous.'

'Afraid you'll look like a complete idiot in front of all those people?' laughed Joe.

'What if I make a mistake? What if I come in at the

wrong time? In the wrong key?'

'One, you won't,' said Doug. 'You're a good musician. Two, if you hit a bum note, you can correct it on the next and then you're fine again.'

'Three,' said Joe, 'they're RAF boys so who gives a fuck what they think?'

'Four,' added Terry 'this is ENSA. Expectations aren't high.'

Lights dimmed. On stage, the show started. Whistling, cheering, booing, screams. There is nothing a group of young men relish more than making childish noises in the dark. Our MC for the evening, a fat man in a tuxedo, walked on into the spotlight. More cheers, shouts of 'hide the grub'. He gestured for silence. The dying noise gave someone the space he needed. 'He's had more hot dinners than I've had hot dinners.' Laughter again, smothering his introduction. Not our problem. All we cared about was our twenty minutes. We were on third after some old woman assaulted the *White Cliffs of Dover* and a beard in a suit gave it *As Time Goes By*. Doris, who seemed in charge backstage, approached us. 'How do you want announced?'

'Good point,' said Terry. 'We don't have a name.'

'Aye we do: The Joe Robertson Trio.'

'Since when?'

'Since now.'

'I'm not sure about that name.'

'What's wrong with my name?'

'Not your name. The band name.'

'What's wrong with it?'

'Well, it's not very democratic is it, naming it after only one member?' I said.

'Never liked democracy. One man one vote? I've met some men. I wouldnae give them a fright if they needed a shit, let alone give them a vote. We can't call it "The Joe Robertson Jack Thingy and Terry Taffy Trio" can we?'

'Any other ideas?' Terry said.

'How about Viva Joe Stalin?'

'How about no?'

'If you're going to use anyone's name, it should be Jack's,' said Doug.

'What?' I said. 'No.'

'The Jack Trio? That's a bit shite, isn't it?'

'No, his surname. The Devine Trio. Devine, like divine. Holy, spiritual, wonderful.'

'He's no holy, spiritual or wonderful,' said Joe. 'The only holy thing about him is the one he speaks through.'

'No, it's a pun, you see? Devine. Divine.'

'I need something now,' said Doris.

'We seem to have two suggestions,' said Terry. 'The Joe Robertson Trio or The Devine Trio, which is a pun, apparently. Hands up for the first.'

Joe raised his hand. Then he raised his other hand. I thought it was a bad name, but I didn't want my name to be used, so I voted for Joe. 'And votes for the second.'

Terry and Doug raised their hands. 'A draw.'

'Hang on,' said Joe. 'He's no even in the band.'

'But the name was his idea,' said Terry.

'What do we do now?' said Doug.

'Ask her,' said Terry turning to the woman. 'Should we be called The Joe Robertson Trio or The Devine Trio?'

'Which one of you is Joe Robertson?'

'He is.'

'And is one of you divine?'

'I am,' I said.

'You are that, love,' she said with a salacious wink.

'Vote cast,' said Terry, as I turned bright red. 'The Devine

Trio it is, at least for tonight.'

'Fucking democracy,' said Joe.

Only three of us, so there was nowhere to hide. I was way over at the edge of the stage, space between me and them. I thought back to the club in London, to those GIs. They were relaxed, didn't even look like they knew the crowd was there. It was them and the music. Maybe that was the trick. Ignore them. I closed my eyes. Stepped closer to centre stage. I was back in the big field, sitting on the thickest branch of the oak tree, sun setting after the day's work. The birds, the beasts, the distant sounds of Dod cleaning his boots, smacking them off a rock to dislodge the dirt. Thwack. Thwack. One, two, one two three four. G G G G, G G D, keep it simple, keep it basic.

Hot ginger and dynamite. One note, the next. First verse, chorus, verse, chorus, instrumental, verse, chorus, verse, chorus. End. That noise. I'd never heard it before, not rushing at me like that. Applause. I opened my eyes. Looked back at Joe. Next song. He winked, one, two, one two three four. Middle C, F, A. The dots in my head, the lines and clefs, the time signatures. Followed them with my mind, followed Joe and Terry with my instinct. Eyes closed again, concentrated on the music, lived inside it, wrapped myself in it. This, Jack, fucking *this*. Over too fast, four songs, twenty minutes, *Straighten Up and Fly Right.* Time for the next turn. The crowd were disappointed. We bowed, they cheered. We were a hit. There was much back-slapping backstage. No idea who was on next. Didn't listen. We didn't care. More whisky. The ATA girls had come and Terry and Joe got stuck straight into chatting them up. I should have gone and talked to Rose, she stood like a spare next to Doug and Mavis, but I wanted to be alone, to bask in my memories. I'd done it, a gig. I'd played jazz on stage, in front of real people. I found space against the wall, sat on the ground with my trumpet in one hand and the whisky in the other. We went out after, the eight of us. So they told me.

Sunday, zero nine-hundred hours, standing at the start line, hungover.

'Well Terry? Thought of anything?'

'Nothing.'

We'd gone a mile and I'd been sick twice. The other runners had disappeared into the distance. Terry was looking for somewhere we could hide, keep out of sight until they came back and we could rejoin them, when a mechanical scream knocked us to the ground.

Eighteen bombers, three groups of six flying low. Guns going and it was just like before, everyone was thinking it. But they roared off overhead and we could breathe again. Relax a little. A truck stopped. Jimmy, face white. 'Get in. Bombed the church. A tip and run raid. The dirty fucking…' He was choking up, the anger in him. 'The church.'

The church. Sunday. Too far. Too fucking far. The church down in rubble, gone, just the tower standing, the steeple, and around it all these people, crying, screaming. We rolled up and were straight in to help with clearing the rubble. There were people under there. Kids. Kids under there. Fucking Sunday school, wasn't it? Right in the middle of Sunday school. Some were alive. The feeling. Rocks pulled back, what was once a pew, shards of glass, and there was this little girl, no more than seven, and she was fine, a bit dirty, crying, but not a scratch on her. The feeling of it, the energy it gave me to keep digging, to keep moving masonry. But it wasn't all like that. There were bodies, course there were. Carrying a comrade's body back was one thing, a grown man, a volunteer, no matter how he died, but that? A wee boy, a wee girl, life smashed out of them, body broken, soul gone, and you knew somewhere behind you there were parents waiting for news, hoping and praying, watching other families reunited, and you knew you'd got to carry this little bundle that used to be a future out to them, that was the hardest, that was the thing, the thing that hardened you, the thing that made you want to get straight out there and find Jerry and get revenge. But there was this voice, this thing inside that nudged you, saying this is what it's about, Jack, this is what you're training to do. Would you do it, Jack, in a Lancaster over Dresden, over Frankfurt, indiscriminate bombing? A Sunday school in Leipzig? Would you, Jack?

Twenty one futures snuffed out. Three Sunday school teachers. And when everyone was accounted for, good or not, and we were washing the dirt and the blood off our hands, then more news. And we didn't want to hear it, not more news, but it was Jerry. One of them clipped the steeple of the Catholic church, flying too low, and crashed into the town.

Running. Running so hard and fast to get there, to get him, to get hold of him and rip him apart then drag him to see his handiwork, to see those little bundles and to look at the mothers and fathers, to make him apologise, to make him beg for forgiveness and to refuse to grant it, to send him straight to hell with the curses of humanity, but of course, when we got there he was dead. They were all dead, and revenge would have to wait. We left their bodies for the townsfolk to deal with. As we rode in the truck back to the base no-one spoke. No-one could. What could we say? When we got back others wanted news, they wanted stories, was it true? Kids? And one crashed? But no-one could talk. Only one thing to do. We were dismissed, told to get ourselves cleaned up. Terry had another bottle of whisky and we went down the beach, threw off the unclean uniforms, the dirt and dust. Blood. Naked and clutching the bottle we walked into the sea, waves washed it away, whisky washed it away, in silence we got drunk, tried to forget.

We each locked ourselves away. Days passed. Weeks rolled on. Clouds thinned. Days passed and no-one really noticed. Maybe the town was cursed. All that carnage in such a short time. Heads down. Books. Marching. PT. Just didn't think about it. All we could do. Life went on, though no-one knew how. News said aircrew deaths to date. Axis: 18031. Allies: 9906. We were winning but it wasn't enough. Statistics and rage. Different worlds.

Storms break. Fog shifts. Mists lift. We moved out of minor keys, let brief motifs of light in. The odd joke, a smile. The fire within each of us was rekindling. Fiercer now, but warmer too. We made it back to the heat.

A long queue outside the greengrocers.

'What's happening?' I asked a woman near the front.

'Oranges, love. They've just got some oranges in.'

'Oranges? Really? I haven't seen an orange for years.'

'None of us have, love, but a shipment got through and Albert here got hold of some. Listen, why don't you go in ahead of me and get some?'

'Oh no, no, I'm all right.'

'No, lad, I remember you. You were at the church. You can go on ahead.'

'No, you've as much right to an orange as anyone else.' The people behind nodded, friendly, gestured for me to go forwards. The uniform was useful for getting drinks in pubs, that kind of thing, but this was different. I backed off, thanking the woman, but she wouldn't hear it. Manhandled through the door, pushed up to the counter, emerged with four oranges, all against my will. I couldn't eat them. I tried to think of a way to send them home, let Lizzie and my folks taste them. Maybe they'd go off, or get lost. In the end I gave the lot to the woman who ran the hotel as a thank you for letting us play music in the hall. Terry disagreed.

'You did what? You got four oranges and you gave them away, just like that? Have you gone soft in the head?'

'Why? What was I going to do with four oranges? I get enough to eat in the mess. They don't.'

'That's not the point. Do you know how much they're worth? We could've given them to the girls. Dear God, we'd have been right in with those. Give the girls an exotic present like that and you'll be behind the bike-sheds before you can say "knee-trembler". Use your loaf.'

'Life isn't all about getting behind the bike sheds.'

'Not for you. If I don't get any off Winnie, I'm blaming you!'

Exam time. The four of us studied together, no longer me helping Joe, all of us helping the others, being helped in return. I tested myself. Theory of flight. Air movement, lift, updraft, downdraft. Drag. One force meeting another force, the contortion of space by the movement of the aircraft through it.

Meteorology. Fluid mechanics. Weather systems. The movement of air. On a farm, the ebb and flow of life is controlled by the climate, the seasons. Knowing exactly when the weather will break, when to plant, when to harvest, when to take the beasts inside, when to shear. A day too late and the crop was ruined; a week too early and you'd run out of feed. In Scotland there's only one thing you can say about the weather: it's changeable.

Navigation.

Aerodynamics.

The hours. I studied for forty-five minutes, took fifteen to smoke, stretch, then back to it. Start with the difficult, identify problems, move onto the easier, back to recheck the difficult. Do it again. And again.

Two or three nights a week we'd pack it in early, play some music. At the weekends we'd go drinking. Sometimes we'd see the ATA girls, sometimes not. Terry was smitten, Joe always up for it. Doug and I sometimes went along, sometimes cried off, walked along the cliffs instead. It was a beautiful summer, but the beach had been spoiled for us. No-one could enjoy swimming without looking towards France, keeping an eye out for those black dots. We were nearing the end of our time in Babbacombe. When our training was done at the end of July we'd be off to flight school, an actual airfield with actual aircraft – if we passed. The news, the final confirmation sharpened everyone's motivation. Complaints about the workload ceased altogether, tiredness was worthwhile if it meant getting into the air. This was what we'd been after all along. One evening, a couple of weeks before we were due to leave, as we were going over our Air Force Law notes in the hotel bar, the owner, Mr Sutton, came over. 'Sorry to interrupt, lads, but I was wondering if you could spare a moment?'

Doug shifted over so Mr Sutton could pull up a chair. 'The wife and I,' he said, 'we've had this idea, you see, and wondered if you would we be at all interested, of course there would be no money in it, what with the RAF in our hotel, money is hard to come by, I'm sure you understood that, but the bar would be put at your disposal, as long as you are reasonable with your, ahem, consumption, but if you are agreeable with these terms then would you mind awfully providing the music for a dance?'

'A free bar?' said Joe.

'A dance?' said Terry. 'With girls?'

'Yes, and yes,' said Mr Sutton. 'Though both within reason.'

'We'd love to play,' said Terry. 'Thank you for asking, and thank you for letting us practice here. Playing at your dance is the least we could do.'

'When?' I said. 'Only we have exams coming up.'

'Oh, I know. When do they finish?'

'July twenty-second is the last exam,' said Doug. 'We get posted on the twenty-sixth.'

'Let's say the twenty-fourth, then. The Saturday night?'

'Perfect,' said Joe.

'Mister Sutton,' I said. 'It's only been three weeks since… the church. Are you sure it wouldn't be… insensitive to have a dance?'

'It's good of you to consider the town like that, son, but trust us. It's just what everybody needs.'

'Well, if you're sure. The last thing any of us want to do is offend anyone here.'

'Good. It's settled then,' said Mr Sutton. 'I'll set about promoting it.'

'Make sure you promote it in the St Vincent's,' said Terry. 'It won't be much of a dance if there are only RAF lads here.'

'Oh, don't worry,' he said. 'Some of the local girls will be sure to come as well. It's been a while since we had a proper dance in this town.'

'Local girls?' I said. 'We'd better get practising.'

'Aye,' said Joe. 'And we need tae get word tae those ATA girls, get them over.'

'They'll be there,' said Terry. 'If only we had some fruit

to tempt them with.'

Classes stopped. We studied all day, practiced in the evening. Word got around. Everyone was talking about it. Anticipation and excitement filled the Babbacombe air for the first time in months. ENSA was all very well, but this was special. Although it would be full of military people, it wasn't a military event: There was a fair chance it wouldn't be awful. Our four-song set needed to be much bigger. We set about rehearsing any song we could think of, including some of Terry's own tunes. Terry spent his free time in front of the mirror practicing his crooning look. I'd been thinking a lot about the kind of jazz we heard at the club in London. I had no idea what it was called, but that faster, more complex style attracted me. I tried to recreate it but it was like trying to describe a dream. It was never on the radio and there was no-one in Babbacombe to teach me. Still, I could feel my style changing slightly. I loosened my grip on the trumpet, relaxed my body. Stopped picturing the notation in my mind. They were barriers, frontiers, prison bars. The main thing I remembered from London was the fluid way the saxophonist and the clarinettist approached the rhythm. They seemed to slide around the beat, notes drifting. I'd always imagined the beat like hitting a nail with a hammer: if you're not bang on, you're going to break something. But what if the groove came from relaxing that strictness?

The exams were much harder this time. We'd learned more and needed to prove it. Four days of papers and practicals, Monday to Thursday. By Thursday night we were nervous wrecks, the stress of the exams, the dance. We walked out of the last exam and straight into the pub. I was legless in under two hours, pouring the stuff down my throat, had to be carried home. Friday I wanted to die.

Vomit. Headache. Never again. After parade, the results. Joe, Terry, Doug and I all passed. Doug and I got pretty good grades, Terry good enough, Joe just made it. On Monday we'd be off to No. 29 EFTS Cliffe Pypard, Wiltshire for our basic flight training. Flight. We'd made it.

'Pint to celebrate?' said Joe.

'Excuse me.' I ran to the toilet.

I felt much better on Saturday, but the nerves had multiplied. Four songs at ENSA was one thing, but this was us, all night. Terry got confirmation from Winnie that they'd be there. Before the guests even arrived we began to partake of our free bar, steady the nerves, relax the music muscles. No-one spoke.

It was time. Doug gave me a pat, reassurance. Slow steps up to the stage. I kept my back to the crowd, focused on Joe's kit. Mr Sutton announced us, The Devine Trio, and we were go, drum roll please, adrenaline, Joe tapping his sticks, one two three four, and we were off, all aboard the *Chatanooga Choo Choo*. Feet moving, bodies swaying, the dance was underway. This was music, jazz, life. Sweat pouring off us, refilling as often as we could, and in front of us the townspeople and the military presence danced like the end of the world was nigh. Our set was structured very simply, two fast, one slow, repeat. Build them up, bring them down, build them up again. *Nagasaki* upped the tempo. *Body and Soul*, *Stardust*, *Honeysuckle Rose*, *Take the 'A'-Train*, *Boogie Woogie Bugle Boy*, *Rum and Coca Cola*, *Straighten Up and Fly Right*. We finished the first half with Terry doing his best Glen Miller on *Moonlight Cocktail* and then it was a quick run to the toilet for all musicians, followed by a refill at the bar. We couldn't believe the first half was over so fast. I'd only just blinked, drawn breath and it was half over. I was itching to get back up there but

Joe and Terry were happy to have an interval. The girls had come. 'You guys are amazing,' said Mary to Joe.

'Ta very much,' he said. 'You're no bad yourself.'

'They need two bands,' she said. 'So you three can get a break and come for a dance.'

'She's got a point,' Terry said. 'We're not going to get a dance at all.'

'Jack and Joe can,' said Doug. 'Terry can accompany himself, give the lads a break.'

'What about me?' said Terry.

'Well, just trumpet and drums won't be much to dance to.'

'Jack can manage that,' said Joe. 'Bit of Satchmo.'

Just me and Joe. No Terry. Me centre stage. Alone. Drink. 'Why not?'

'Great,' said Terry. 'I'll go first so you two can dance, then I'll dance with Winnie here. We can rotate.'

'You and Winnie can rotate?' said Joe.

'No, we can. We can take it in turns to have a break.'

'Done.'

And so we did. The night unfurled. The band got drunk; the dancers got drunker. While Terry was onstage alone, I danced with Rose, the feel of a body, her body, contact as we moved around the floor. Spinning, images twirling in me, Rose, the music, being on stage, the girls at The Windmill. My head on her shoulder, the smell of her hair. Something in me, like romance, some wave of something but what's the point? Off soon. Contact is enough, alone, together. A tap on the shoulder, back onstage. Joe danced with Mary. I spotted Clive, clearly very drunk, crossing the dance floor. I caught Joe's eye, nodded. Joe manoeuvred Mary into position, at just the right moment spun her with one hand and felled Clive with the other. He was dragged off the dance floor and thrown out the fire escape. We played more. We danced more. I got so drunk I could barely stand and blow at the same time so I sat on the edge of the stage, my legs hanging down. We exhausted our repetoire so went round again. I was in a different key from everyone for about ten seconds before I noticed and moved up half a tone. Terry disappeared out the fire escape with Winnie and came back with an ATA cap on. Eventually, we couldn't play another note, did *The King* at speed, got off stage and topped up our already full alcohol tanks. Doug and I took Mavis and Rose onto the dance floor where we waltzed to imaginary music. I buried my head in Rose's hair, held her close as we swayed around the room. Everything was spinning, the lights and the music, the kaleidoscope. Joe and Terry disappeared with Mary and Winnie. Clive came back demanding revenge, took a swing at Doug, missed and hit Paddy. Paddy hit him back so hard he upended a table covered in empty glasses, and a proper fight broke out. Punches were flying, officers got what was coming to them, glasses smashed, drink splashing. Doug and I, Mavis and Rose joined the other four at the fire escape. 'Gentlemen,' said Terry. 'Our work here is done.'

'Do you think we're ever going to get through a gig without a fight breaking out?' I said.

'Not as long as Joe's in the band,' said Terry.

The fire doors swung closed behind us as we went two by two into the darkness.

Another train, rattling from Torquay to Swindon. In London there'd been hundreds of us. In Babbacombe the numbers had come down. Now we were in groups of twelve, each posted to a different Elementary Flight Training School. A dozen. You can't hide from each other. Certainly not on a train. Ten of us in the same carriage, Pete and Chalky in the baggage car with the kit. The band wasn't split up, but Clive was with us. He and Joe were tied at one sucker punch each. Maybe it would be over. A draw. A truce. No chance. We were bored. Smoking. Swapping papers, magazines. I spy. Cards. Smoke. Inhale. Exhale. Tick.

'John Wayne's real name is Marion,' said Terry.

'Aye? Marion? That explains a lot,' said Joe.

Terry was flicking through old magazines and newspapers, trying to find something, anything of interest. He rolled his head, like he was stretching his neck, trying to ease a strain. 'Frank Sinatra isn't in the Army,' he said. 'Doesn't say why.'

'Maybe he's in the Navy,' I said.

'No, he's not in the military is what I mean.'

'He's got a good voice,' I said.

'It's all right,' said Terry. 'Bing Crosby is better.'

I remembered I had a letter from Lizzie. I'd picked up my mail but with packing up and shipping out of Babbacombe, I'd shoved it in my pocket unopened. 'Oh, a letter is it?' said Malcolm. He'd been in Doug's flight group, so we'd never really met until the platform. 'A girl back home?'

'Hey, Jack's got a dirty letter,' called Bill, another new face.

'Better not be,' I said, 'it's from my sister.'

'You dirty sod,' said Malcolm.

'Fuck off.'

'Here,' said Bill. 'Where's that letter you got, Malc? The one from whatsername.'

'Lily?'

'No, the other one.'

'Ah, Babs. You're not seeing that one. You'll go blind.'

I slit it open, tuned out of the banter. Paper must be getting short at home, Lizzie had written on blank pages ripped out of a book.

Dear Jackie, I hope this letter finds you well. You did not say in your last letter when you would be leaving Babbacombe. Life on the farm continues much as usual. Mother is convinced that someone is stealing her cigarette cards and Father only comes in for tea and sleep. The ditch in the bottom field has collapsed in but he does not have the strength to sort it himself. Hope you get some leave soon, there are hundreds of jobs waiting for you.

I have been volunteering in the hospital two or three days a week. They do not need me, but you know what it is like. It is not too bad, a few other girls from Inverayne are there so it is a laugh, sometimes. I have some bad news, I am afraid. Willie Rennie is in the hospital, recovering. He is not bad – I mean,

*he is not critical - but he lost his right leg. He was in Tunisia
and got hit by a mortar. He has been in hospital in Edinburgh
but they have transferred him here before he goes home. Mrs.
Rennie is in every day. Apart from the leg, he is fine. Healthy,
anyway. He is not talking much. Maybe you could send him a
letter? He just sits there all day, staring at the wall. Write back
soon, tell us where you are. Have you played any more gigs? I
am writing this outside. It is lovely today, Mother's roses are
beautiful.*

    Take care, Jackie,
    Your loving sister, Lizzie.

'You alright?' said Terry.

I swallowed. 'Aye, fine.'

'Bird given you the elbow?' said Clive, giggling.

'You, shut it,' said Joe. Clive stood but Bill pushed him
back down.

'A mate,' I said to Terry. 'Back home. Lost his leg.'

'Fuck.' The joking, the posturing stopped. 'Where
abouts?' said Joe.

'Tunisia. Mortar.'

Another one. The list getting longer. Not dead though,
that was something. Fuck. Willie? I remembered him
alongside me, up a tree, stepping from branch to branch,
jumping into the rhododendron bushes, sinking to the
ground. I'd write to him. We should get leave after Swindon,
I'd go see him. And say what?

The Tiger Moths were lined up waiting for us. We hadn't slept well the night before. It was like Christmas morning; learning to fly. Every moment of childhood joy. Impatient yearning. Tripping over the steps, our eyes on the kites. Desperate to get our hands on them. We settled behind yet more classroom-like desks and tried to keep our focus on Thor. We'd encountered him briefly the day before. It was his job to decide which of us would become pilots. This man was our God, sitting in judgement. All through the training in London and Babbacombe we'd known this moment would come, when we'd meet the decision-maker. Thor didn't disappoint. Named for his muscular build, his blond hair and thick moustache, Thor was officially known as Pilot Officer Olsen. If a civilian walked into the room, someone who knew nothing about rank and insignia, he would instantly assume Thor was the boss. He never had to demand respect. That casual confidence of a leader. This was the RAF we'd been imagining, the service we'd volunteered for. Kites, big moustaches and complete command of the skies. Tally ho. 'This, gentlemen, is the Tiger Moth, our primary trainer, and she is a beauty. The work of Geoffrey de Havilland who was an amateur lepidopterist, hence the name. Before you leave this airfield you will have fallen head over heels for her. Twenty-three feet eleven long, wingspan twenty-nine four, powered by the totally efficient Gypsy four-cylinder a hundred and thirty horsepower engine. This little darling has never ever failed in mid-air. A range of approximately three hundred miles and capable of climbing to thirteen thousand feet at a rate of six hundred and seventy-three feet per minute, you can do what you like to her and she'll take it. Throw her about, fly upside down for minutes, she'll come out of any spin or dive with a minimum of fuss and you can bang her into the ground on landing and she won't break. Which is why we let you loose in her. By the time you leave here, some of you may be permitted to go on to become pilots. This is where we separate the wheat from the chaff, boys. Twelve hours of flying and then an assessment. If you pass, you will become a pilot and go on to fame and glory. For those of you who show sufficient aptitude, you will be asked to fly solo at a time of your instructor's choosing. Flight Sergeant White, please.'

White took his cue and dished out thick, square books bound between two hard, blue covers. A face of mangled skin and scarred flesh, one eye bulging violently out the socket. One of the civvy girls told us later he'd had to crash land and his kite ran into the petrol depot. He was lucky to be alive, though clearly he wasn't grateful: From the moment we climbed down from the train in Swindon, he'd been hectoring, insulting and punishing. We called him The Face.

Books handed out, The Face returned to his spot along the wall next to Flight Sergeant Graham. Thor continued his address. 'This here is your log book. Guard it with your life. It never leaves you. Every second you spend in the air is written down in this book. If you lose it, I will personally hunt you down and do something imaginative and nasty to you. It is more important than your rosary, more important than that photo of your little darling, if it is a choice between losing your balls and losing your log book, you will sacrifice everything you hold most dear.

'I will be instructing some of you. Others I'll have little or no contact with. I wish you all well. If you listen, learn, and leave your cockiness on the ground, we will begin the long process of turning you into deadly weapons. There is nothing more lethal to the Nazi than a Royal Air Force pilot in a Spitfire, and if you do what we tell you, exactly as we tell you, there's no reason why that can't be you. 'Now, Flight Sergeant White will assign you to your instructors and then we will proceed to the first flight.'

His job done, Thor left the room in charge of White. He took the stage, rubbing his hands. The atmosphere changed. 'Right you lot. You may think you've learned a lot about flying with your head in the books at ITW and your pre-pubescent dreams of downing Jerry but I'm here to tell you that you know nothing. Flying is not about weather forecasts or lines on maps. Over the next few weeks we're going to teach you enough not to destroy His Majesty's aircraft. We'll see if any of you actually have what it takes to be a pilot. I doubt it. Every month we get a dozen like you, and every month we send back bomb aimers and navigators, a dozen boys so inept as pilots that they'd help the British war effort more by joining the Luftwaffe. Now, I suppose, by the law of averages, we have to find a pilot one day, but as I look at you lot here, today, it will not be this month.'

By now we were used to these spirit crushing speeches.

No-one listened.

Willie. I wanted to write to him, but what do you say?

The Face got round to doing his job. Doug, Pete, Chalky and I were with Thor. Joe, Bill, Sandy and Clive got Graham, and Terry, Malcolm, Danny and Frank got The Face. No-one reacted openly, but inside there was considerable cheering or swearing. We were to wait there in the crew room until called. Bill, Pete and Danny were up first. 'I tell you one thing,' said Terry. 'At least with him sitting in front of me, I won't have to look at that face.'

'Second against the wall,' said Joe. 'I'll take great delight in putting that bastard against the wall when the revolution comes. But only after that cunt there.'

Clive gave him the fingers.

Joe jumped up, his chair flying out behind him, clattering into the wall. Clive didn't flinch. I thought for a moment Joe was going to go for him, but it looked like he was going to stick to threats for the moment. Not going to get into trouble this close to his first flight. They'd circle each other, but neither was going to make a move. We had little to do but wait. Terry suggested cards but we were unsure of our footing and The Face would be waiting to catch us out. The room offered little in the way of entertainment. A wooden hut filled with wooden chairs and desks, a blackboard, a light and some windows. The dark wood soaked up the light and it felt like late afternoon, even though it wasn't even nine o'clock. Doug rose and walked over to the window. Outside stood the Tiger Moths, three of them were taxiing out in a bumpy line. Even under the control of the instructors they looked like young birds hopping along for their first flight. 'Away, away, for I will fly to thee,' Doug said. Others came over to join him and we watched the first three complete a circuit: Up, four lefts, down, out and back to the crew room.

Bill and Pete came in with big smiles, already walking the walk. Danny looked pale, the contrast with his jet black hair making it even more pronounced. Thor patted him on the back and looked around the room. 'Thirty minutes alone and not one of you got a pack of cards out? You're not going to last long as pilots if you don't learn to fill the time, lads,' he said.

'Sir,' said Terry, producing his pack in a flash, appearing like they'd been in his hands all along.

'Preparation is the key,' said Thor.

The next three were called. I was one of them.

Perched on top of my parachute trying not to think about why it was there. Remain in control, focus the mind. The mind wouldn't focus, birling off in every direction. Every nerve tingling, every sense primed. I was ready. Time. Focus. Focus on Thor's broad back. Through the rubber communication tube he was outlining the pre-flight routine, the checks to make, the things to remember, focus on that, listen, Jack, listen. 'There isn't much to it, Devine,' he said. "There are so few controls and dials, but the important thing isn't the utility, it's the habit. The kite doesn't move an inch until everything has been checked and rechecked.' Check, Jack. Recheck. 'On the left we have the engine revolution counter. Next is the air speed indicator which indicates air speed. Follow?'

'Yes, sir.'

'Below that is the cross level so you can fly straight. Then there's the altimeter which shows your height and the small one is the oil pressure gauge.'

Revs, speed, level, height, oil. 'Righto, Devine,' said Thor. 'Grab hold of your joystick. Move it sideways. See the ailerons moving? They control the angle of bank in a turn. Move it forwards and back and it raises or lowers the elevators. This makes the nose go up or down. Pull back, we go up. Push forward, we go down. Rudder you control with your feet. Speed is controlled by the throttle here, open or shut, and this is the ignition switch. Up for on, down for off. Questions?'

Questions? Is your stomach doing this as well? Were you like this the first time?

'So I check the chocks are in place, turn on the ignition and ask Doris to kindly start the prop.'

A girl in civilian clothes swung the prop and it took, sending violent vibrations through the kite and through us. Only my clenched teeth didn't rattle. 'I will have control throughout the flight. Is your stick locked?'

'Yes, sir.' I held my breath. We shuddered forward, taxied into place.

'Ready?'

Not even slightly.

'Ready, sir.'

Rolling along the strip, picking up speed, concentrate, Jack. Don't yell, don't scream, don't do anything to embarrass yourself, don't get classified LMF on day one. Lacking Moral Fibre. A coward begging to be taken back down. Or reckless, yahooing like a drunk cowboy. These are all things that just aren't on. Not done. Not cricket. Calm, in control. A RAF pilot. I tensed. Up. Airborne. Flying! Seconds, metres dropped away, untense, relax, think that maybe I was all right. I was supposed to be watching the instruments, learning how this kite flew, because in a few flying hours I'd have to do it myself, but the outside of the kite pulled my attention. Outside. In the air. My God, in the air. The freedom: this was what I'd been dreaming for years. All the waiting; All the marching; All the studying. High over the Wiltshire fields. Greens and blues and yellows. Smell of the fuel, feel of gravity. Eyes over the gauges: Fuel, altimeter, horizon, speed. Lifted my sight to the cloudless sky, sun on my left. Remain vigilant. There's a war on, you know? Thor was saying something. 'Sorry, sir. Could you repeat that?'

'I said, how are you doing back there?'

'Great, thank you, sir.'

'Not queasy?'

'No, sir. I'm enjoying it very much.'

'Good boy. Don't mind if I make it a bit more interesting, do you?'

'How do you mean, sir?'

'Well, our brief is "straight and level flight". A tad boring all that.'

'You're the boss, sir.'

'Good lad.'

Goodbye stomach. Distance between arse and parachute, straps straining. Bite lips to avoid any sound escaping. This is a test. Numbers rolling down and down towards zero. We levelled out far closer to the ground than I thought safe and buzzed over the forest, treetops within reach. Sharp turns, banking, thrown about, this way and that. Do birds feel like that? Acknowledge the g-force as they spike and curve? Tiger Moths were nothing but canvas and wood and that didn't seem nearly strong enough to withstand that kind of treatment. But withstand it, it did. Thor brought us up sharp and spun the kite around. Hanging upside down, kept in only by straps, the sound of the engine dying. We coasted along.

'All right back there?'

'Yes, sir. Sir, I thought Gypsy engines never failed?'

'They never do. Unless you fly upside down.'

'Oh.'

'Don't worry. Watch.'

We spun the right way up and immediately the engine kicked in.

'The fuel can't get into the engine. Once it can there's no problem.'

'I understand, sir.'

'Good lad.' We landed and Thor showed me how to fill in my log book. Thirty minutes flying. Duties: Familiarity with Cockpit Layout; Preparation for Flight; Air Experience. Patted me on the back. Enough moral fibre to be getting on with. And that was it, my day over. We spent the rest of our time chatting, telling the stories of our first flight, comparing, contrasting, embellishing, exaggerating, covering up. Chalky had thrown up. The rule was 'you throw up, you clean up'. From that day on, no-one ate much at breakfast or lunch.

Besides guard duty and flying, our time was free. The invasion of Sicily had begun, and we caught all the news. Willie should've been there, his regiment named. The RAF bombed Rome for the first time. We all cheered that, envious.

Machine gun nests dotted around the base needed to be manned, but since nothing much ever came over, we'd tune in a radio and bask in the sun listening to the latest tunes. We kept our attention on the skies. Everyone worked under the assumption that Jerry knew we were there, what we were doing, and may decide that untrained pilots on the ground were easier targets than fully-trained pilots in a Spitfire. We knew what Jerry would do given half a chance. Well, he wasn't going to get even half a chance again. Not when we had machine guns and orders to fire. We secretly hoped Jerry would come on our watch so we could get one back. No exams for the first time in months. Flights were about thirty to forty-five minutes a time, once or twice a day depending on weather and rotation. Since we were only allowed up in perfect conditions, the weather became our main topic of conversation. Life was getting comfy. Terry practiced one-handed card cutting, one-handed shuffling, tricks that made him look like a pro card player, moves that might unsettle other gamblers. I was pretty sure I caught him rehearsing some dodgier skills, like dealing from the bottom of the deck, but I wasn't sure and wasn't going to mention it. I spent a lot of time in the library. Joe took one look at the library, dismissed it as 'imperialist propaganda' and settled down with *Capital* and a determined expression. He knew he'd never get through it and that if he did it wouldn't be in full understanding, but Alec'd told him to learn, to keep bettering himself, and by Christ that's what he was going to do.

I got to take control. A loop round the airfield but it might as well have been intercontinental. Once you were up the instructor handed over control. You turned to port, then flew straight a bit, port again then reduced speed, handed back control and came in to land. Straight and level flying, climbing and descending went into the log book. The Tiger Moth was easy to fly; difficult to fly well. A swing prop so the propeller had to be started by swinging it round by hand. This was done by local girls who worked on the base and was a dangerous job: some lost hands. A cruel thing, to make them do it. Back up in the air. Lighter, buoyant, unshackled and soaring. Nerves on the runway, dropping away, just that moment, the present tense, time held still, the absence of tick, the second before a wave breaks, when it hangs. Britain from above, God's eye view, the base below, moving south from us, the land stretching out north and east, rolling hills, green and pleasant land. Heading north, my horizon filled with peace. Reminded of Doug talking about what the world would look like if there were no people, what it had looked like before we'd come along with our buildings and cables and roads.

A sudden noise startled me. I jumped slightly and knocked the tube to the floor. It was Thor attempting communication. What had he said?

Sounded like, 'You have control.'

I scrambled about trying to retrieve the tube so I could reply. The kite dropped and I was lifted into my straps. I couldn't reach the tube. Every time my fingers touched it, it slipped away. I could feel the kite tipping, diving, beginning to spin.

Caught the tube, got it up and back into place, wrenched the stick into position, adjusted the throttle and pulled her out of the spin, textbook. Straight and level. Breathed. Took hold of the tube.

'I have control.'

'You amaze me,' said Thor, his tone reprimanding but not angry.

I took her back to a decent altitude. 'Now,' said Thor. 'Breathe.'

I exhaled, re-entered the moment. 'Keep your eyes on the instruments,' said Thor. 'Don't worry about outside. Always trust your instruments. If the artificial horizon says you are level, then you are level, regardless of what your senses tell you. You can be tricked. The kite can't.'

'If I'm in a dogfight, sir, then I can't watch my instruments.'

'True, but by the time you get into a dogfight your

kite will be as much a part of you as your own arms. You won't need to do more than glance at them. For just now however, concentrate on the dials.' Keeping her level was tricky and needed constant adjustments. I was amazed at how bumpy it was up there. The main problem was the sensitivity of the controls; the slightest nudge could send the kite careering across the sky. At times it felt like riding a bicycle over a ploughed field. I was glad of the protection of the parachute underneath me. One Instinct that had to be fought by anyone who'd ever driven a car or a truck was to treat the rudder pedals like brakes. We'd been warned more than once on the ground not to 'stand on the brakes' since we wouldn't stop, but we might go into a spin. I'd only driven a couple of times so I didn't have that instinct to fight. I did however have to overcome the urge to pull back on the controls like they were the reins of a horse. All that did was send us leaping into the sky. I banked, levelled out, banked again. Slowly I relaxed, let just my fingertips guide the stick and she responded, smoother and smoother. We'd been up for thirty minutes but it felt like a matter of seconds. I was beginning to get the hang of her.

'Right,' said Thor. 'I have control. Lock your stick. To land, first you begin the descent, and reduce airspeed slowly. Not too fast. If you slow too much we'll drop out of the sky. The aim is for us to reach that point inches above the runway.'

I watched the dials, the dropping of airspeed and altitude. I knew the theory, the danger of stalling if airspeed disappeared, but this wasn't a textbook. You had to judge the distance and calculate the rate of descent, the airspeed needed to bring us down exactly. You had to keep her level so she did a three point landing, bringing both wheels and the tail skid down perfectly at the same time. It was pretty tricky but it was considered a poor show to land two-point. A mark against.

'Well done, Devine.' said Thor. 'Your first flight in control. We'll have you taking off and landing soon. If the weather holds we'll get you up again tomorrow.'

Buzzing. I vaguely heard Thor, like he was underwater. As I walked back to the crew room I drowned in adrenaline. I'd done it. It was like music.

I had a day off and was back up the day after. New duties for the log book: Medium turns, gliding and climbing turns. Over the weeks we were to do spins, stalls, forced landings with the engine cut, side-slip and land in a cross-wind. As I read each one, I tried to imagine myself doing it. Thor's calm, strong voice and the rising confidence from each successful flight. When a mistake happened and Thor had to step in or sharply order me to do something, to correct it myself, I tucked the lesson away, did it again, got it right, two in a row. I knew they were testing my ability to learn, to adapt. I had to be flexible, open, I had to know the kite inside and out, know how she'd react in any given situation, know how to counter any sudden change. Thor usually let me struggle through whatever mistake I'd made. 'You have control,' he said. 'But don't stray too far. We'll just run through the basics. I don't like the look of that front.'

Deep, dark storm clouds curled over the horizon. I ran my eyes over the dials, over my surroundings, over the dials, over my surroundings. 'When you check your surroundings,' said Thor, 'you must remember to check the ground as well as the sky.'

Why had he said that? Had I missed something? I scanned the ground for anything unusual, something I should have seen. Ah, there it was. A chequered flag. Flying cancelled.

Land. I moved her into position. 'You have control,' I said, preparing to lock the stick.

'No, I don't,' said Thor. 'You have control.'

Had I done something wrong? Had I misread the flag?

'Take her down, Devine. You can do it.'

Making a mistake at ten thousand feet was one thing, making a mistake at ten feet was a lot more serious. Try not to think about the ground. Stalling. Crashing. Failing. 'Gradually, air speed and altitude, straight and level, breathe Devine, you have to breathe. Bring both wheels and the tail skid down together, straight and level, that's it, that's it. Touchdown.'

There's an area. Most people never notice it, the space between the land and the sky. It's not like a line, a border where one stops and the other begins, rather there's a place where you're still in the sky but under the influence of the land. It feels like gravity is heavier, stronger. At ten thousand feet you're free to move any way you want. In those last feet it's magnetic. Every pilot knows that tension, the fight for control as you approach. It's like passing from one world into another, through some special zone between. The first time you fly through it, it scares the bollocks off of you. A little wobble, reduced speed, taxied to a halt. Exhaled. The swagger that took me back to the lads after landing was more pronounced than ever. I'd fucking landed.

The storm front moved in and parked itself over us. There'd be no more flying until it shifted. We played cards, tried to chat up the women that helped around the base. They did everything from start the kites to serve food in the mess, but most of them had been working there for a year or two and were more than used to the way RAF cadets thought. Even Terry tried only half-heartedly, more as a way to pass the time. He was still pining for Winnie in Babbacombe. They'd promised to write. *We'll Meet Again*, was about hope, not reality. Four years of war had taught us all that no, you probably wouldn't meet again, even if you both survived.

I wrote to Willie, threw it away. Useless words.

Terry and I spent hours in the mess playing the tunes Terry seemed to write with endless ease. Joe was getting mouthy with us. I tried to think of a solution, boxes, dustbins, anything, but nothing suited Joe. I mentioned the problem to Terry.

'Hard luck,' was all he offered.

'You're not worried about the band?'

'I'm worried about him. He's going to do something, probably to Clive, and I don't want to be anywhere near him when he does.'

I didn't think it was that bad. Joe hated Clive and would never forgive him for the first fight, for beating him, but beyond another fight, there was little Joe could do. And Clive was ready for him. Neither would get to sucker punch the other again. The storm may have grounded us but it didn't interrupt guard duty. We cycled in three groups over three nights to keep the Tiger Moths safe from sabotage or paratroopers. We were dropped at dusk beside the kites, a mile from the camp, and abandoned. No phone, no form of transport, just us, a rifle with bayonet and no ammo. The first night of the storm was our turn.

A windy night and cold, so we huddled together in the lee of a hut. The rain was holding off but we expected it back any minute. The wind wasn't giving up. We stayed close to shelter, a technical breach of regulations but no-one cared and no-one would find out. Only the most sadistic of officers would bother getting out of bed in the middle of the night and coming out into a storm just to catch us. Still, we kept an eye out for officers just as much as for Jerry.

'This reminds me of home,' I said. 'Of school holidays.'

'Really?' said Terry. 'You spent your school holidays guarding Tiger Moths with a rifle? I must've I had a pretty sheltered upbringing.'

'No,' I said. 'I mean being out all night with my pals. There's a forest behind my house, mostly rhododendrons, ash, beech, but enough bigger things like oak that we could make proper tree houses. We'd a whole sequence of walkways, thick branches tied together so we could get across large sections of the forest without ever touching the ground. We built platforms, swings, things like that. We'd play hide and seek, war games, the usual stuff.'

'This was when you were, what, sixteen, seventeen?' said Terry.

'Ha ha. No, ten, eleven.'

'Sounds terrific,' said Doug. 'There are no forests around us, just the odd copse. They've all been cut down for building or for clearing farmland. All our games had to be played in the open. War games are pretty boring when there's nowhere to hide but face down in the mud.'

'We used to do it like football,' I said. 'You know, two captains, pick teams, keep score. My brother Dod and I were always the captains. Our forest, we knew it best, so it was always us. Against each other. We'd play capture the flag, or manhunt. Games would last for days. During the summer we'd sometimes go on all night.'

'Your parents let you play out all night?'

'It was only dangerous if the Lord was having a shooting party. Then we had to stay indoors.'

'My Da never worried,' said Joe. 'Alec and I stayed out most nights, hanging round the closes, getting intae all kinds of trouble, trouble with the law, trouble with other boys, gangs, trouble with fathers of daughters. Da never gave a fuck. Always far too drunk. Suited him. Suited us. If we werenae there he couldnae hit us. If we werenae there he could forget about us.'

'When you were ten or eleven?' said Doug.

'Aye. Alec was a bit older than me and I was always with him, except when he was with a lassie. Mind you, that was most of the time. Until he got intae the politics. Then it was lassies half the time, politics the other half. Sometimes meetings, sometimes handing out pamphlets, selling papers, sometimes a proper scrap with the Fascists. Good days.'

'And you were always with him?' I said. 'Even in the fighting?'

'Course in the fighting. A man's gottae learn tae fight sometime, and where could be better than with his big brother against the scum of the fucking Earth?'

'I never spent much time with my brother,' said Doug. 'He was always off somewhere else, travelling, visiting friends. He hated Yorkshire, being so far from "culture". He was away at boarding school and only came home briefly during holidays. Then he left school for university and trips to the continent. Then the war started and he joined up. I've only seen him once since thirty-nine.'

'He's in the RAF?' said Terry.

'Yes. Lancasters.'

'He's commissioned?' said Joe.

'Yes.'

'Your family rich then?' said Joe, in that tone.

'No. Edward got the last of the money, nothing left. I went to the local grammar and then signed up. No university or foreign jaunts for me.'

'What did your old man do?' I said.

'He owned a woollen mill,' he said, keeping an eye on

Joe, who muttered something that sounded like *means of production*. 'But it went bust.'

'Why?' said Terry.

'His mill became uncompetitive because he wouldn't cut costs. You see, his competitors were laying off workers, bringing in more and more machines, cutting wages, increasing hours. My father wouldn't do that. The mill had been in our family since his grandfather, and most of the workers had been there for generations too. It was like a family. The mill paid for schooling for the worker's children, paid for doctors when they got sick. Looked after them, you know. They helped us so we helped them. Well, you can't make money that way, not in this day and age. But he wouldn't change. He wouldn't let them down. In the end he had no choice and it went under.'

'Sounds like a good man,' said Joe.

'Thanks,' said Doug. 'But I don't think it was anything special. It used to be like that around us. All the mill owners looked after their own. But times changed and look what happened. You can't make money as a good man.'

'True,' said Joe. 'But after the revolution it'll all be different.'

'You've got a brother and all, don't you Terry?' I said.

'I do, yes.'

'Older?'

'He is, yes. He's a miner, protected occupation, so didn't get called up.'

'You didn't want to be a miner as well?' said Joe.

'No,' said Terry. 'I mean, I should've been. All planned out, isn't it? Miners in my family as far back as anyone cares to remember, which admittedly isn't far, but you know me, I'm not one for doing what others tell me. So, on my eighteenth, when Gareth was preparing everything for me to join him in the pits, I ran off to the recruiting office and signed up for this malarkey. The names he called me. You'd think I'd signed up for the bloody Luftwaffe. Still, it was signed and sealed and nothing he could do about it. RAF got me first. Much rather be up in the air than underground. Both'll kill you but the view's better up there.'

'I was the same,' I said. 'Signed up without talking to my folks. I mean I'd have gone anyway. Farming's only protected if you're over twenty-five. But after losing Dod, my mother was never the same.'

The wind was picking up, making conversation more and more difficult. We drifted off into our own worlds of reminiscence, lost in the past. 'What's that sound?' said Doug, after a few minutes.

We listened for a moment but the swirl was so loud it was hard to tell even the direction sounds were coming from. 'Nothing. It's just the wind,' I said.

'It's not just the wind,' said Doug. 'I know the wind. It doesn't sound like that. The low thrumping is the wind. What's that creaking?'

'My back,' said Terry. 'I need to get into a warm bed. Or a warm woman. Preferably both.'

'That's definitely not the wind,' said Doug and began pacing, stepping off in different directions trying to triangulate the sound. I could hear it now as well.

'That noise,' I said. 'I think it's coming from the kites.'

'I think you're right,' said Doug.

We walked over to the planes, guns ready, though no-one really expected to find a saboteur at work. 'It's the wind,' I said. 'Look.'

I pointed at the planes. The noise was the wind battering the canvas and wood bodies of the Tiger Moths. They were taking a hammering like a ship in a storm. 'That's can't be doing them any good,' said Terry.

'It's not,' said Doug. 'I think we're going to have a—'
Before the word 'problem' was even out of his mouth one
of the Tiger Moths took an especially strong gust under the
wings, lifted up and flipped over.

'Shit,' said Terry. We dropped the rifles, useless against
wind, and ran over to the wreckage. 'Why is it when we're
on watch that things go wrong?'

Two of the other kites were lifting off the ground. Doug,
Terry and I ran to one, hung onto the wings, trying to keep
it grounded. Joe ran to the other and grabbed the propeller.
Us three were winning but another big gust lifted Joe's kite,
him still hanging onto the prop. 'Fuck! Help!'

'Let go, for fuck sake let go,' I shouted.

He did, dropped back to earth. The plane continued
over onto its back with a crunch. Another started to go,
I joined Joe and we held that one down. We had no rope,
no way of tying them down, all we could do was run from
plane to plane, forcing it back down, trying to beat the wind.
No sooner did we get one down than another went. We
hung onto wings, wheels, whatever it took to keep it down.
Sometimes it wasn't enough. By the time the wind finally
shifted, six kites were on their backs, wheels up like dead
insects. The ones we'd kept the right way up were damaged
where we'd been hanging on. There wasn't one plane that
would be able to take off. 'Well done us,' said Terry as we
surveyed our night's work. 'Jerry doesn't need to bother
with paratroopers, he just needs to wait for a windy night.'

'I'm telling you,' I said. 'Canvas and wood are no good
to make an aeroplane.'

Luckily Thor was the first officer on the scene, not The
Face. Thor agreed with Terry's assessment of our work but

understood that realistically there was nothing we could've done to prevent it. The Face would've torn a strip off us, had us cleaning the runway with a toothbrush, but Thor outranked him, so he had to settle for barked orders and a general demeanour of anger. Everybody was grounded for a few days while they repaired the planes they could and replaced the others.

Now there was no hope of flight for a while, the military swung into action devising ways to fill our time. A competition was organised with a local Home Guard unit. Us twelve against twelve of them, capture the flag over a decent expanse of the Wiltshire countryside. 'Your mission,' said Captain Duncanson of the Home Guard, briefing us, 'is to find and capture the flag that my men will be defending. The rules are simple and they'd have to be for you RAF types to understand. The flag is in one fixed location, guarded by my men. You must find it, secure it and return it to your commanding officer by any lawful means necessary. The area is defined by these landmarks,' he pointed to a map. 'You must remain within these boundaries. If you stray over a frontier, you are deemed to be dead and may take no further part. If you die, you must return here immediately. If someone points their rifle at you and says bang, you are dead. If you point your rifle at someone and say bang, they are dead. If you point your rifle and don't say bang, no-one dies. If you say bang without pointing your rifle, no-one dies. Once you are all dead, or you have the flag, the mission is over. Any questions?'

'Sir,' said Terry. 'What happens if I point my rifle and someone else says bang?'

'Nothing.'

'Sir,' said Joe. 'What happens if one of your men points his rifle at me but I say bang?'

'Nothing. Now—'

'Sir,' I said. 'What happens if I point my gun at someone and they point their gun at me and we both say bang at the same time?'

'You're both dead. Now—'

'Sir,' said Doug. 'What happens if I point my rifle at myself and say bang?'

'You get court-martialed. Suicide is not an option during war. Now stop asking stupid questions. The mission will begin at zero hundred hours tonight.'

'Sir,' said Terry.

'What is it?'

'Is there a time limit?'

'You have twenty-four hours.'

We waited until his back was turned then pointed our rifles at him and said bang.

We sat in the mess drinking weak milky tea, plotting. We decided to split the twelve of us into our guard groups and each try to take the flag individually, cover more ground that way. On the table Doug, the brains of the operation, had placed a map, the game area divided into thirds. 'Start and end at midnight,' I said. 'The darkness will be the best time for us. Four men can hide much more effectively in the dark than twelve.'

'Hiding isn't an option,' said Terry. 'They stay still. We have to find them.'

'If they're even in our sector,' said Doug.

'If they're not, this is just going to be a decent walk in the country,' I said.

'Good point.'

'Jack's right,' said Joe. 'We've a much better chance of sneaking up on them while it's dark.'

'Look at the map,' I said. 'These two areas are wooded, along the riverside is open. Open land is much more dangerous during the day, so I say we work our way along the river, cover half the exposed land from zero hundred until dawn, stick to the woodland while it's light—'

'Find somewhere sheltered, have a kip,' said Terry.

'Good thinking,' said Joe. 'And finish the rest of the riverbank after sunset.'

'Sunrise is about half past five, sunset just before nine,' said Doug. So we prepared. Rations, binoculars, whatever we thought we'd need. At zero hundred Thor sent us off with the words, 'do us proud, lads.'

Our sector was the farthest from the camp. All twelve of us left together, Danny's group breaking off first, cutting across a fallow field. Then Chalky's lot, ducking off the road into the forest. It was a dark night, the moon frequently behind cloud banks. We walked in silence. After forty minutes we reached the bridge that marked the beginning of our sector. We climbed down and took shelter under the stone arch, one final check before the hunt began.

'Last smoke until dawn,' Terry said, lighting up, hand cupped over the end. 'Won't be seen under the bridge.'

In the brief flare of the match I noticed something. 'Where's Joe?'

He wasn't there.

'Was he with us all the way?'

'I thought so,' whispered Doug. 'He was at the back. Definitely behind me when Chalky's group broke off.'

'And after that?'

'I don't know. Once we were in the trees it was too dark to see. I could make you out in front of me, Jack, just, but I couldn't even see Terry up front.'

'Hold on,' I said. I climbed out from under the bridge and raised my head above the stonework, waited until the moon came out. The road was empty.

'Joe?' I hissed. Nothing. Back down. 'He's not there.'

'Oh, fuck,' said Terry.

'Do you think we lost him?' said Doug. I looked at Terry.

'No,' Terry said. 'He went with Chalky's lot.'

'With Chalky's lot? Why?' said Doug.

'Clive,' I said. Joe was technically AWOL. All we could do was go on with the mission and hope he showed before midnight.

We covered a lot of ground quickly, although we couldn't make out much. We'd have to stand on top of the flag before we could see it. No sign of Joe either. Spread out, talking only when necessary, we swept half the riverbank then worked our way towards the tree line, reaching it as the sun came up. Exhausted, we found a secluded spot and crashed down. Nibbling at our rations, we spread the map out, marked off what we'd done.

'How long do you reckon to do the forest?' said Terry.

'About six hours,' I said. Doug nodded agreement.

'Fine,' said Terry. 'Let's get some kip, set off again at ten, rest again at four, final search after dark.'

'I'll take first watch,' I said. 'An hour then change?'

'Do we need a guard?' said Doug. 'We're looking for them, not the other way around.'

'If I were in charge of the defence,' said Terry, 'with a dozen men just sitting around, I'd send out scout groups.'

'Fair enough,' said Doug. 'I'll go next. See you in an hour.'

They settled down, I looked around for a good guard position. The forest was pretty dense, visibility a couple of metres at best. I found a likely tree, climbed up. Much better. I could see along the river, across the open land. If anyone came through the forest they'd be on us before I saw them. Nothing I could do about that. At least this way I could narrow down the possibilities. I took a sip from my canteen, lit a fag. It'd been a long night and I could do with some sleep, but the rule for guard duty was the same as Terry's rule for buying beer: be the first, then it's done and you can relax. I checked my watch. Nearly seven. Time to climb down, take a quick scan of the area then wake up Doug. As I shifted my weight, lowered my leg to the next branch, something caught my eye. I froze, but the tree swayed. I prayed it looked like wind. It was a man walking across the open land between us and the river. He was coming in our direction, not straight for us, but near enough. Moving gently, I got the binoculars out. Joe. Strolling along, rifle slung over his shoulder like a pick axe. I checked all around but couldn't see anyone else. If they were close, they'd see him, but maybe we'd get lucky, maybe they were nowhere near. I climbed down, picked up my rifle and made my way to the tree line. I stepped out for a moment. He saw me, I darted back into the trees. He changed his direction, sauntered over.

'Morning, Jack. Any tea on the go?'

'Where the fuck have you been?'

'Oh, took a wrong turn. Had tae wait until it was light tae find you. I don't have the map, you see.'

His smile, smug grin, clearly lying. I wasn't going to push it though. I was tired. 'Come on, we're through here.'

I was about to wake Doug for his watch, when a thought occurred. 'What did you do while you were lost?'

'Nothing, why?'

'Just curious. Did you, say, move around? Do anything?'

He was trying to see what I was driving at. Obviously he'd done something, didn't know what I knew.

'No, nothing.'

'Good, so you're well rested then. We've been searching this area all night and are knackered. You can take the watch until ten.'

I didn't wait for an answer. I thought he'd argue, so I just lay down, put my cap over my face. Spark of a match, footsteps.

Doug shook me awake. At first I was groggy, lost, thought I might be back home, the forest behind the house in Inverayne, then I remembered. Doug packed up his rations and got ready to leave. Joe and Terry were both sitting on fallen trunks, smoking. Neither was looking at the other. 'Do you need to eat anything?' said Doug.

'No, I'm fine,' I said. 'Let me take a piss and we can get going.'

I had to keep reminding myself this was an actual military exercise. It felt so much like playing manhunt back home. Dod and I both had our tactics. He liked to stay low: ditches, shrubs, ground-brushing trees. There were a few places where a seemingly solid wall of rhododendron bushes were thin enough to pass through. I knew most of them, Dod knew them all. He could appear beside you like a ghost, disappear just as easily. Height was my friend. Smaller, lighter than Dod, I'd learned to move around amongst the top branches. A dense forest, much like this one, with intertwining limbs, I and the wee lads following me could cross huge sections of woodland without ever touching the ground. No chance of those tactics in Wiltshire. I'd grown a lot since those days, and Dod's game plan seemed more suitable. We swept through, tree to tree, stopping, listening, signalling with hand gestures. When we set off from the camp, Terry was withdrawn, one of his cynical moods, Joe no doubt. The Swindon road was our first check point, and we reached it without incident, cut south a couple of hundred metres and began to make our way back to the river. This criss-crossing of the forest meant we could be reasonably sure to have covered the whole area and end up precisely where we needed to be at sundown. Once we were clear of the road, we stopped for a rest. I sat with my back against a sycamore, ran my hand down the bark, rough and warm, thought of the oak in the big field back home, thought of sitting on the bough blowing soft jazz into the sunset after a hard day at it. Doug rubbed at his neck. Joe stood next to me, ripped a plate of bark clean off, whitish-green underneath. Got his knife out and began carving. 'Why are you doing that?' said Doug. 'That tree never did anything to you.'

'Just a fucking tree. No a fucking human being.'

'What's *No Pasaran*?' I said. Joe had carved it into the tree.

'Spanish,' he said. '*No Pasaran.* They shall not pass.'

'I didn't know you could speak Spanish,' I said.

'Ah cannae, just that.' Slipped his hand into his pocket where the scrap of flag Alec had given him was. '*No Pasaran,*' he said again, quietly.

'You're a fucking nutter, mate,' said Terry.

'Fuck off.'

'Fine, you're not a nutter. So where did you go this morning?'

'I told you. I got lost.'

'Just happened to get lost at the same time as Clive. A total coincidence.'

'Watch it, Taffy,' said Joe, the knife still in his hand.

'Why? You going to stab me? That what you did to Clive?'

'Last warning.'

'No, your last warning. If we get back and anything's happened to Clive. I'll be the first to turn you in.'

'You turn me in for anything and I'll do you in, is that clear?'

'Boys,' I said. 'Keep the voices down. We're supposed to be on a mission here.'

'On a mission, Christ sake, Jack,' said Terry. 'It's not important.'

'Aye, that's you, Taffy,' said Joe. 'Nothing's important, not us, not the war, not anything but yourself.'

'And you're so different?'

This was going to escalate.

'Right,' I said. 'Enough. Let's get moving, sweep the forest and get to the next rest spot and wait for darkness. Standing here fighting is just stupid. Let's go.'

'Fuck off, Jack,' said Terry.

'Aye, fuck off, Jack,' said Joe. I shook my head, started walking. They followed.

We found nothing in the forest, and were pretty sure our sector was empty. A waste of time. I realised we had no way of contacting the other groups. If we found the flag it would be twelve against four. The other eight were effectively out of the game. Splitting into groups when we were all hunting the same target was really bad planning. Was that Thor's teaching technique at work? Letting us fail by ourselves, allowing us to make mistakes in order to learn from them? We should've asked his advice. We still had one area to check, the second half of the river. 'Christ, I need a drink,' said Joe.

Night. We made quick work of it. Nothing. We crossed the river into Chalky's area. It was only twenty-two thirty hours, still an hour and a half. 'Let's cut across country,' said Doug. 'Make our way back to the base through the mission zone. You never know, we might find something.'

We'd all much rather have walked along the road than across fields, but Doug was right. We couldn't pack it in early and I couldn't be arsed hanging around waiting yet again. It was as good as over, though. No-one checked the map, we just kept trudging south, not trying to mask our sounds. Joe had a fag and no-one bothered to stop him. Beyond the last field lay another wooded area. As we approached a sudden voice: 'BANG!' Three figures stepped out, rifles raised. For a moment I panicked that we'd been mistaken for paratroopers and would be shot, then I realised they wouldn't say 'bang'. 'Oh, fuck off,' said Terry.

'Got you. Never light up at night, matey, gives you clean away.'

'What dae you think you're playing at you stupid English cunt! You could've given us all heart attacks. What you daein running round in the dark with a gun for anyway? Don't you know there's a war on?' Joe was squaring up, but Terry spoke first.

'Hold up a minute,' he said. 'You said "BANG!"'

'What you babbling about?' said Joe.

'I did,' said the Englishman. 'Who did you say it at?'

'This one here, the short fighty one.'

'Thought so,' Terry said, and ran off into the forest.

'Come back here you bloody coward!' shouted Joe. 'Never run away from a fight. Right, that's it. When I'm finished with these three, you're getting it too.'

The three Home Guard looked around, unsure what to do. Should they follow Terry or stay with their prisoners? They had rifles but carried them like they might go off any second. One of them said, 'So, should we off these two and get after him?'

'Off us?' I said. 'You can't do that. We're Prisoners of War. Only he's dead,' I gestured at Joe. 'For him, the war is over, so he can go back to base. But you have to take us with you to your base. We're POWs until zero hundred hours, until the exercise is over.'

'Fuck off,' said one. 'Take you back to base? Think we're daft?'

'If you shoot prisoners during this mission, we'll report it.'

'Balls,' said the third. 'He's right. Fine, let's go and no funny business.'

We left Joe to make his own way home, but I guessed Terry wouldn't be too far away. If he had any sense he'd have gone about ten metres into the trees and then hidden. Doug and I crashed our way through the undergrowth making as much noise as possible. Maybe he could follow us and get the flag. 'Will you two fucking stop that,' one of our captors said.

'What you going to do? Geneva Conventions, lads,' I said. 'We're untouchable.'

'Listen, pal, even under the Geneva Conventions I can still give you a clout round the head and claim it was a branch. Now shut up.'

Of course, we didn't. Soon we came to the defence base. Sure enough, we'd wasted a day: It was right in Chalky's sector. I wondered if they'd been found. Doug and I sat on the ground while the army lads argued about what to do with us. Judging by the amount of people all for offing us, I'd hate to be an actual paratrooper caught in Wiltshire. They finally decided they couldn't do anything. The scouts set off on another patrol, leaving us with a guard of five. They were positioned around the perimeter, looking out. 'What time is it?' I asked Doug. 'Quiet, you two,' someone said. We ignored him. He managed to find some moonlight. 'Twenty-three twenty-seven.'

'Almost there. Can't wait for my bed.'

'You know,' said Doug. 'When pilots are captured by the enemy, it is their duty to try and escape. All across Europe men are trying exactly that.'

'Good point,' I said. 'And it would be awful of us to refuse to do our duty.'

The flag was on a pole in centre of the camp, which was set up in a small clearing. It was only a few steps to the trees. The guards were all looking out, and with a bit of luck I could be past them and into the forest before they realised. 'You grab it,' said Doug, 'and run. I'll get in the way here.'

'Okay.'

'Wait... wait... now.'

I ripped the flag from the pole and took off at full speed, cleared one soldier lying like a sniper, jinked behind a tree, then another. I had no idea if I'd been 'shot' but I wasn't stopping to find out. Once enough trees were between me and the base I ducked behind a fallen trunk and listened. Nothing, but any pursuers might have stopped as well. I checked the time. I needed to get moving if I was going to have the flag back at base. Another listen. Nothing. Jogging this time I made my way out of the forest and onto the road. I didn't have time to go cross-country. I ran down the road, hoping my luck would hold and the night would hide me. No chance.

Round a corner and a soldier walking towards me. He

reacted first, gun up. I stopped, panting, hands in the air. Suddenly a clatter. His gun had gone and there were now two figures. 'BANG!' 'Fuck!'

'Jack, run,' said Terry. 'He's dead.'

I ran, made it back to the base moments before midnight. Joe was already back, as were Danny's lot. 'Everything all right, Devine?' Thor said.

I was out of breath, couldn't speak. Slowly feeling came back into my legs and my lungs opened up. 'Well, Devine,' said White. 'Running from a spooky monster? Afraid of the dark?'

'No, sir,' I panted, and took the flag out of my jacket.

Chalky's lot arrived at zero thirty-four, Terry and Doug with them. 'We found the base,' Chalky said, 'and then you two turned up. We didn't know what to do so we waited. You nearly landed on me running out of there.'

I looked around. 'Where's Clive?' Terry looked at me, eyebrows raised, shook his head.

'With the MO,' said Sandy. 'Cracked his head open.'

I looked for Joe. Couldn't see him.

'How?'

'No idea. Must've fallen. He was the last man. We heard a noise, turned back, he was on the ground, blood pouring out his skull. We bandaged him up best we could, took him back here.'

The three of us, we said nothing.

New kites had arrived, flying back on. Now we were into the fun stuff. We had time to make up so we went up every day, sometimes twice a day. Terry had The Face as an instructor but maintained he wasn't as bad in the air as he was on the ground. 'He's in front, you see? So he can't see me and I

can give him two fingers all day long. And when he starts
going off on one I can just drop the tube and suddenly I
can't hear anything. I tell you, going to and from the kite, it's
complain about this, complain about that. When he's off on
one I'd love to just pop him one in the mouth, shut him up
for five minutes. If I ever got him in a dark alley, boy I could
have some fun.' Joe walked into the mess. Terry walked out.

'How's Graham as a teacher?' I asked, wondering how
this was going to end.

'He's fine,' said Joe. 'A big softy really. Getting on a bit.
He flew in the first war. You know they used tae drop bombs
with their hands? They just leant over the side and let them
go. It's a long way from that tae the Lancaster.'

'I'd rather be in a Lancaster than in a Camel with a box
of bombs on my knees.'

'He's a great one for the stories,' said Joe. 'He was telling
me about this instructor, real public school boy, the accent
on him most folks couldnae understand. He had these three
boys up in an Oxford, learning how tae use the bomb sight.
They swore they'd heard him say "jump chaps" and did.
All three parachuted down and made their way back tae
base. Turned out he'd said "pump flaps". Washed the three
of them out.'

My log book filled up. Mnemonics: HTMPFFGG –
Hydraulics, Trim, Mixture, Pitch, Fuel, Flaps, Gills and
Gyro. BUMPF. Duties: Familiarity with cockpit layout,
preparation for flight, air experience, effect of controls,
taxiing, straight and level flying, climbing, descending,
stalling, medium turns, gliding and climbing turns, take off
into wind, approach and landing, spinning from a straight
glide, low flying, restarting the engine in flight, action in the
event of a fire, forced landing, side slipping, steep turns,
taking off. Day by day the hours stacked up, one hour

twenty minutes, two hours fifteen minutes, three hours forty five. We got through our seven hours' assessments. Clive was out of the infirmary but not cleared for flying yet. I went to visit him.

'Any idea what happened?' I said.

'None. I was walking along, trying not to lose sight of Sandy's back, when bam, like an explosion in my head and I woke up on the ground.

After the assessments the training continued. I went up three times on the thirteenth and once more on the fifteenth. It was all consolidation, me in control throughout the flight. I could take in the dials with only a quick glance, and could scan the skies, even while upside down, without taking her off level. As we taxied to the end of the runway after the last landing, Thor said, 'bring her around for another go.'

I'd happily stay up all day long. I got her in position and was just about to open her up when Thor climbed out. 'Sir?' I said, knowing what was about to happen. 'On you go,' he said. 'You're ready. Just take her round the circuit. Don't do anything fancy. And don't bend her.'

Solo. Going solo. Oh shit. Shit. There was no going back, no getting out of it. If you screwed up your solo that was it. LMF. Stop thinking, stop thinking. You can do this. She began rolling. I took a deep breath, tried to clear my mind. The buzzing was back. The adrenaline. Then we were off the ground and everything changed. I was up, alone in the sky.

The sound of my heart, the blood pumping around my body. Quiet enough, solitary enough that for once I could hear myself. That beating, it's me. That rushing, it's me. Those creaks and groans and sighs, the click in the knee, the growl in the belly, alone in the darkening blue high above the Wiltshire fields.

'Beautiful,' said Thor. 'Couldn't have done better myself. Take the rest of the day off. Here's a pass. Go and get pissed.'

Thor was a great teacher. I did exactly what he said.

Doug also went solo and got a pass. We hitched into Swindon, had an egg and chips dinner, into the Crown and got stuck into the beer. It was just the two of us. For the first time we felt like our uniform wasn't some costume. We'd flown solo. Sure it was only for twenty minutes in a Tiger Moth over Wiltshire and not in battle, but it was enough to give us a swagger which the beer only enhanced. We had a game of darts, both of us useless, and then returned to our perch at the bar. 'Thor told me,' said Doug. 'He had a lad about three months ago. He was doing fine so he sent him up for his solo, only he got scared. Couldn't land. He flew around for about thirty minutes, round and round, but wouldn't come down. Eventually he flew up to ten thousand and jumped out, parachuted down. Would rather jump than land.'

'I'm glad you didn't tell me that until after I'd gone solo. Assuming we pass the twelve hour assessment, we're nearly done here.'

'We're nearly done here whether we pass or not,' said Doug.

'Leading Aircraftman Jack Devine. I like the sound of that.'

'Don't get ahead of yourself. If you're not expectant, you can't be disappointed.'

'Indulge me,' I said. 'If we pass we're likely to be shipped off overseas for the rest of our training. Where do you think we'll be sent?'

For the last couple of years it'd been too difficult to properly train new pilots in Britain. There was a shortage of airfields, aircraft and trainers. So the government set up the Empire Air Training Scheme and sent new pilots to places like Canada and Rhodesia to do their training, free from the Luftwaffe. 'I heard some people get sent to America. That would be something,' I said. 'Imagine being in America. The music. The movies.'

'I'm not sure if I'd like America. It seems so bright and busy. Noisy. Rhodesia might be nice.'

'I don't know anything about Rhodesia. It's in Africa, isn't it?'

'Yes. That's about all I know too. That's one reason I'd like to go. When else would we ever get the chance to see Africa?'

'When would we get the chance to see America?'

'But Africa seems so exotic.'

'Don't dismiss home. I was like you once. Wanted travel, adventure. Desperate to see the world. Then I thought I'd never see home again.'

It was another man, sitting on the stool next to me.

'Sorry?' I said, turning to face him.

'Just saying,' he said. 'Don't be so desperate to get away from home. Alf,' he said, offering us his hand. We took it. He'd been hunched over his pint so we hadn't properly taken in his uniform.

'You're a pilot?' I said.

'Not any more. They've got me behind a desk now. On account of this.' He nodded at an empty sleeve.

'You were shot down?' I said.

'That I was,' Alf said. Doug got a round in, and one for Alf. 'I was flying Lancasters. Got shot down. Ack ack. Don't remember much. Lost my arm in the initial blast but me mate Harry got me out. Threw me out the door and pulled my chord. Used my chute to dress my arm when we got down. How I didn't die I'll never know.' He raised his glass to Harry. 'He got us to the coast, got a fisherman to take us out, did a swap over to a British trawler at sea. Got home. I was out of it most of the time. Lost blood. Delirious. The others didn't make it.' He toasted the air again. 'Never flew again.'

I bought him a pint this time. 'Cheers lad. So, as I said. Don't be so desperate to get away, because one day you might find yourself desperate to get back.'

We talked for a couple of hours, always Doug and I buying. That's what you did. He told us all about real flying, about battle. He'd flown everything, bombers, fighters. 'Always have a knife, lads. Big bloody knife. Keep it in your cockpit. You get shot down, you're going to need that. Defend yourself. Get food. Make a shelter. Look.' He slapped a huge hunting knife on the bar. 'Never leave home without it.'

'My brother says the same,' said Doug.

'He's a pilot?'

'Same as you. Lancasters.'

'Good man. What's his name?'

'Edward Newton.'

'Don't know him.' He raised his glass to Edward Newton.

We got back just after eleven, the buzz from going solo still with us. The next day we were rough, but Thor gave us a day of rest. We felt we'd earned it. Lying on the grass, sun burning off our hangovers, watching the kites flit around overhead. Joe ran over.

'Hey lads, guess what?'

'The war's over?'

'No, just done my solo.'

We jumped up, shook his hand. 'Damn,' I said. 'Shame he didn't send you up yesterday, we could all have gone out.'

'No chance of getting a pass for tonight?' he said. Shook heads.

'You enjoy yourself though. Check out the Crown, not a bad wee pub.'

Doug and I had an early night. We were both back up the next day, more solos. We wanted to be rested and ready, prove it wasn't a fluke. Nevertheless, we were woken just before midnight by Clive, Sandy and Bill coming in drunk. They'd been celebrating, too. 'Fuck sake, boys,' said Terry from under his blankets. He hadn't gone solo yet. Joe's bunk was still empty. With much giggling and swearing the lads got into their bunks and we all went back to sleep. When I woke, Joe wasn't there.

Up solo, the skies to myself. Beautiful, deep green to the horizon, like a model, a toy, me a god zooming over it. I flew north east, over the war games zone. It'd taken us a whole day to walk across the land, and I flew over it in a few seconds. There was an emergency strip on the other side, in case we got into trouble. I felt a bump, rising slightly, falling, hardly registered on the altimeter. I looked, though I didn't need to. The hot air off the road to Swindon. Practiced climbing turns, steep turns. All who had gone solo, we were getting cocky now. I wanted to try a flick turn, suddenly applying full rudder and elevation, flicking the kite through one hundred and eighty degrees from straight and level to straight and level. I was far enough north of the base that no-one would see me from the ground. I checked the sky for other kites. Nothing. Here goes. The first time I tried it my speed dropped too much and I lost altitude, a bit scary, but that's how you learn. I played around with various throttle positions and after twenty minutes of practice had it more or less down pat.

It was Joe's turn in the infirmary with a head injury. Doug and I went in, Terry came in after. 'Walking back tae base last night, had a few, you know, but no a skinfull.'

His breath told the truth.

'So I hear a truck coming on the road behind me and step ontae the grass tae let it pass. I turn tae look, you know, and it's coming pretty slow, headlights full. Well, it gets tae me and I see an arm come out the window and something smacks intae my head. Next thing I know I'm here. MO says it was a bottle.'

'Did you see who it was?'

'No, but I know who it was.'

'So you're even now,' said Terry, arms folded.

'Even?'

'You did him, he did you.'

Joe didn't say anything. Terry waited, his face showing… what? Hope? 'You think I'm going to let him get away with this?'

'Fuck sake,' sighed Terry. 'Joe, just let it go.'

'It's not worth it,' I said.

'Look, Joe,' said Terry, 'listen to me. What's next? Stabbing? Shooting? If Thor found out about any of this the pair of you would be gone before you could say "that was a fucking waste."'

'So you think I should just let him get away with this?'

Terry threw his hands in the air. 'Fine, Joe, fine. You want to pursue this vendetta then you go ahead, but you're not taking me down with you.'

He left. 'You should think about what he said,' said Doug. 'It's not bad advice.'

More flights. Terry went solo. Guard duty.

Waiting.

I put her into a dive and pulled out just to feel the rush. As I was climbing, I noticed another Tiger coming my way. I stopped arsing about in case it was an instructor. It wasn't, it was Terry on a solo. He came alongside, gestured 'follow me'. I checked the time: plenty. No other kites and far enough from the base. What the hell. He banked and I dropped into formation. We buzzed either side of the road to Swindon flying lower and lower. By the outskirts we were at ninety feet. Ahead I could see an old red brick building, about four floors high with a flat roof. Terry seemed to be heading straight for it. Flying over the town meant potentially thousands of people could see us and someone was bound to report back to base. I stayed in formation. We were coming in fast so hopefully no-one would be able to see the individual markings that could identify us.

People lying on the roof. Terry slowed and banked gently so we were circling. Women, I realised, were sunbathing on the roof. Sunbathing in their underwear. Our appearance caused them to scatter like frightened chickens, grabbing at clothing and diving for the door. We did three complete turns then broke off. Terry gave me the thumbs up. I tapped my wrist, he nodded. We split east west so we'd return separately.

Joe was out of hospital and we were on guard duty. After the debacle during the storm we stayed closer to the kites, but the wind was mild, though a light rain started just after midnight. Guard duty was the only time Joe and Terry were forced to spend time with each other. In pairs, checking the fences, the huts, signs of forced entry. I went with Joe, Doug with Terry. Keep them apart. 'Nearly there,' I said.

'Aye, thank fuck there are no exams.'

'There will be though, wherever we get sent for our training. Canada, Rhodesia or wherever. Back into the books.'

'True.'

'Listen, Joe,' I said. 'This thing with Clive.'

'Aye, fine, Jack, aye. Don't go on about it.'

'It's just, I mean, maybe our next posting will have a drum kit, we can start jamming again.'

'I dinnae think that's gonnae happen, Jack. No me and Terry in the same band. Dinnae worry, Jack. You're a good player, there'll be other bands. It's like your first shag,' he said. 'It's the first so it's special, but it's no gonnae be your best.'

'Just, promise me you'll knock this thing with Clive on the head.'

'Fuck sake, Jack. Fine, I promise. Happy now?'

We finished our circuit, went back passed the kites. Joe stopped.

'What's up?'

'Need a piss,' he said. 'You go on, I'll see you back there.'

I shrugged, left him to it. When I got back Doug and Terry were waiting.

'Where's Captain Psycho?' said Terry.

'Having a piss.'

'Let's get in out the rain.'

'Good idea,' I said. 'Where? The hanger or the hut?'

'Hut, it's more sheltered.'

'Right. I'll tell Joe, meet you there.'

'Right.' Off they went. I retraced my steps, couldn't see anyone.

'Joe?' I called out. 'Joe?'

He appeared from underneath one of the kites.

'What you doing?'

'Pissing, I told you. You trying to get a look?'

'No, we're going to the hut. I came to tell you. You were pissing under the kite?'

'On the tyres. Good luck, all the ground crew do it.'

I'd never heard this, but the ground crew were a superstitious lot. 'Come on, the rain's getting worse.'

'Aye. I'm all done here.'

Only two more flights left before my assessment. I couldn't believe it was almost over. To keep flying forever, that was the dream, never landing, never returning to solid ground, stay up there forever.

As I approached the base I was redirected to a different runway. Below me, the wreckage of a kite lay strewn across the runway. Oh shit. Not a crash. Who was it?

I landed, got out as fast as I could, ran over just as the pilot was being loaded into the ambulance.

'Who is it?' I said.

'Clive,' said Bill.

'Clive?' Oh no. 'Is he... he was up solo?'

'Yes.'

'What happened?'

'No idea. His approach was all off, like. Juddering all over the place, up and down, you know? Drunk, looked like. Well, he smacked her into the ground from about twenty feet up, she bounced over, collapsed.'

'Juddering about? Sounds like something mechanical,' I said.

'Yes.'

Clive? Why did it have to be Clive? One image I couldn't

get out of my head.

'All done here.'

The grin on him.

Was it the same kite? No, no, no, Jack. Don't go down that road. Joe's a lot of things but he's not a murderer. I looked around, Terry and Doug, saw them, went over. 'Awful accident,' said Doug.

'Bill reckons it was mechanical,' I said.

'What do you think?' said Terry.

'No idea,' I said. 'I wasn't here.' I couldn't make eye contact.

Joe landed, came over. 'The fuck's all this?' he said, waving at the debris.

'Clive,' I said. 'Dead.'

'Dead?' said Joe. 'Really?'

We all watched his face, watched his reaction. Did we really think he was involved? 'Fuck,' Joe said. 'Shame.'

'Oh fuck off,' said Terry.

'What?'

'Don't give me that. You hated his guts.'

'You saying I had something tae dae with this?'

'I'm saying it's a fucking big coincidence that the very man you vowed to kill is now dead.'

'You'd better have something tae back that up with, pal.'

Terry said nothing. He didn't even know Joe had been near the kites last night. 'Aye, that's what I thought. Well, listen, Taffy. I hear you repeating that tae anybody and I'll fucking come after you, hear me? And if you think I was involved in this, then you dinnae want me coming after you, dae you?'

'You've a screw loose, you know that? Fucking nutter.' Terry walked off.

'How about you two? You agree with that cunt?'

Doug shook his head, held his hands up. Joe looked at me. 'Jack?'

I'd seen him near the kites. He knew that. He stepped right up to me.

'Jack?'

Pause. 'No,' I said. 'Course not, Joe.'

'Good then.' He walked off.

I looked at Doug. He shook his head. This was too much, too fucking much. I began to wish Swindon was over.

Everything was subdued. Another death. We'd seen so many since arriving in London, and still not a chance at combat. How many would die before we got payback? We had a ceremony for Clive, and all kites were grounded for a full inspection. The general theory seemed to be mechanical failure. No-one suspected foul play. Joe kept to himself. Whether he was guilty or furious at Terry's accusation, none of us much felt like being with each other. I lay awake all night wondering what to do. If there was anything I could do. Only three options, it seemed: confront Joe with seeing him under the kite, tell Thor what I suspected, or do nothing. The first would land me in the infirmary, the second would end as soon as I said I had no proof. The third was easiest, but if Joe really had engineered Clive's death, and I kept that secret, wouldn't I then be a part of it? What would a man do? Act? Wait to see what happened?

The kites were given the all clear and I was able to go up. Everyone was nervous, but I wasn't. Seemed I really did think it was Joe; enough at least not to worry about a mechanical failure. Again being in the clouds, feet off the ground, cleared my head. This was my last flight before my final assessment. Turned east and began running through everything I'd learned, then I spotted another Tiger coming at me. Terry again? I thought. I climbed three thousand feet more to get out of the way and to get above the kite, see if whoever it was had an instructor with them. The other kite climbed with me. Dropped a thousand and it followed. Banked steep left. Someone was after playing silly buggers. I slipped north, keeping almost parallel while closing the distance, trying to catch sight of the other man. Two fingers waved at me. Then the face. Joe. Suddenly he disappeared below me, reappeared moments later behind, right on my tail, like in combat. So it was a dogfight he wanted? My first instinct was to ignore him, not to get involved, but fuck it, I thought, I'm not going to let him push me around. I jerked the stick, corkscrewed the kite groundwards, sharply pulled up and spun the opposite way to shake him off. No joy. Opened the throttle and looped over, hoping to get behind him. Joe pulled a three-sixty to the right. Back where we'd started. Over my shoulder. Joe sitting too close so I opened the throttle, put her into a dive, drawing him with me but putting some distance between us. Levelled out, checked our positions. Close enough that Joe would get a damn good fright but far enough apart we wouldn't crash into each other. I pressed down on the rudder and felt the kite slide through the yaw axis, opened the throttle and burst forward, dropping slightly to pass underneath Joe, banking on reflex. Another flick turn, eased out of it and followed Joe's turn square behind him. He slowed down and I came alongside, gave him a 'you're dead' gesture. He returned with a gesture of his own.

I was furious. He was laughing.

Twelve hours done. Once more up with Thor and that was it. I passed. Leading Aircraftman Jack Devine. Officially none of us knew what our final grading would be. There was still the PNB split: pilot, navigator, bomber, but those of us who had gone solo, had done so successfully and had received glowing reports from our final assessment were confident. Not everyone had finished, the weather playing havoc with schedules, so we wouldn't be leaving for at least another week. Terry and Doug had passed but Joe was having a bit of trouble with his final few flights. We'd got away with our dogfight, but he'd got too cocky and nearly stripped the wings off his kite diving her on full bore beyond the two-seventy limit before pulling back on the throttle. Graham tore a chunk off him, something no-one thought was possible, and he had to behave impeccably to pass the final test. He managed it, just.

I spent the last few days lost in myself. I took to sitting in secluded parts of the base with my trumpet, using it as an excuse to be alone. I tried experimenting but nothing was coming out right. Did I really think Joe had messed with the kite? Dates were confirmed. We'd be leaving on the twenty-eighth for fourteen days embarkation leave, followed by regrouping at Heaton Park, Manchester, for final training assignments and shipping overseas. We were done. Next time we got in a kite it would be in some far flung part of the Empire. But we'd still be together. Of the twelve who arrived in Swindon eleven had made it. Just Clive. Leading Aircraftmen. LACs. The camp was awash with newly-made LACs running about with bit of paper, books, cash, doing whatever it took to get the signatures we needed in order to receive the vital railway warrant that let us go on leave. At the station Terry went west, Doug, us two Scots and a few of the others caught a train back to London and then north. At York we said goodbye to Doug. At Edinburgh, Joe and I parted.

'What are you going to do?' I asked.

'First thing,' said Joe, 'is tae hit every bar on Sauchiehall Street, then get myself a wench. It's been too long.'

'It's been a month,' I said. 'Don't you remember Mary?'

'A month?' said Joe. 'Christ, as long as that? You?'

'Work on the farm, I suppose. Not much else to do in Inverayne.'

'Well, see you, have some fun,' said Joe. 'No idea when we're going to get leave like this again. Don't piss it away.'

He started to walk away.

'Joe,' I called out. I don't know why, but I'd started.

'Aye.'

'Tell me,' I said. 'Clive. The kite. The night we were on guard. You didn't, did you?'

I watched his face, the emotions cross it. Anger, fear, hatred. Then a smile. 'Jack,' he said. 'You're a smart lad. So listen tae me. Dae yourself a favour. Dinnae ask me that again, right?'

That wasn't an answer.

'Off you go, Jack. Back to your farm. Straighten up and fly right, Jack. You'll get on just fine.'

The east coast, the green fields, the cliffs, the sands of Montrose and Stonehaven, Dunnottar castle. What would it be like? Late summer the air would be full of insects, the smell of Ma's flowers, the fields a few months shy of the harvest. This was the time for climbing trees, running through fields and being shouted at for messing with the crops. For swimming in the river, dropping in from the big swing, for all-night games. But I'd be doing none of that now. I was going home a man, Leading Aircraftman Devine.

I could forget about Joe for a couple of weeks.

Inverayne, Aberdeenshire. August – September 1943

Left leg in snow up to thigh. Right in deeper, up to top. Seeping into boots. Chilling. Drop pack and sinks out of sight, black hole where it landed. Gone. Already more snow filling hole, erasing what was there, blizzard throwing on top. Swirling wind. Scarf unravelled, whips off, billows away, ghostly. Chilled to the bones. Step forward with difficulty, like some metal machine, raising foot as far as can, falling forward, snow impacting under weight. Make progress, but slowly. So slowly. Feel like will never make it. Never make it to the end of the road, to where the house is, where the home is, home is where the…

Home is where the

Nothing. Three walls. Portion of roof defying gravity. There must be rubble under all that snow. House can't just disappear.

Keep moving forward though seems pointless. Can't still be there, in the cellar under snow and rubble? Must have moved and never told me. Can't wait here. No forwarding address here. Should turn around and leave, go back, back to where come from.

I should go back.

Go back.

Go

I woke with a start, cold sweat, looked around trying to regain equilibrium, find my feet, solid ground. The dream image fading slowly, the snow and the ruined house. Just a dream. The summer sun flowed in through the window. No snow. Just a dream. The house was still standing. Just a dream.

Aberdeen station, bags coming down from the luggage racks, people eager to get off, waiting at the door. I saw the ruined house standing in the snow, the image superimposed on the station as I waited for the next train. Ahead of me the tracks and the opposite platform, but around the edges, around the periphery I could see trees, snow, three walls. Could hear the wind and feel the chill. Stamped my feet and stretched, trying to wake up properly, to shake the dream.

The train pulled in. I wished I had something to read, a *Melody Maker*, Doug's poetry, Joe's *Manifesto*, anything to get my mind off that image. Inverayne. Hard to believe. I leant on the bridge and looked down at the shallow, wide flow. Further upstream the river ran by the end of the bottom field. We'd built the swing, swam when it was warm enough. Me, Dod, Lizzie, our friends. Willie Rennie. I dropped my cigarette end, watched it tumble into the water and disappear. An equation describing the path of a falling bomb. The hill into the village. Laden with kit I hardly broke a sweat. Much fitter. I had two routes, one straight though the centre of the village, past the school, the post office, round by the church and then down the dirt road to the farm, or right, skirt the playing fields, go by McLean, the game-keeper's house, through the big field. I chose the latter, not in the mood to exchange even the briefest of pleasantries with anyone. Fences. Dry stone dykes. Barriers everywhere. They'd always been there of course. Lambs' wool on the barbs. Balance on the dyke. I noticed them now. Demarcation. Most of this land was Southall's. I hoisted my bags higher and spat on the ground. Joe was in my head. That grin.

'I'm all done here.'

'Do yourself a favour, Jack.'

Was he a killer?

'Oh, Jack, we just got your letter this morning,' Lizzie said as she ran over to greet me. I was surprised at how much more like a woman she'd become. I had to count from her year of birth to be sure, but she'd turned seventeen while I'd been away. In my head she was always a little girl, hair tangled, mud under her nails. She looked tired, her blonde hair up, twisted into a bun and caught in a hairnet, arms covered with diluted blood and feathers.

'Chicken for tea?'

'No, I just killed Ma. Want to help me bury her?'

I was home. Thank God it'd been Lizzie I'd met first.

'It's good to see you.'

'You too, Jackie. Let me look at you in that uniform.'

I did a turn for her, then saluted.

'Very nice,' she said. 'It suits you. Better than Dod's old

clothes, anyway.'

'Thanks. How are you? How are things here?'

'Och, you know.'

I followed her. 'As bad as that?'

'Do you really want to know?' She returned to plucking the chicken. I offered to help but she waved me away.

'Well, I'll hear all about it sooner or later, and I'd rather hear it from you than from Ma.'

'Oh you'll hear about it from her right enough. You know her. She'll never miss a good opportunity to complain.'

'So, what is it?'

'Och, nothing specific. Just the usual, times ten. You're not here to help Da and the only boys left in the village are either weak, stupid or both, so hiring is going to cost more. Ma's just the same, only now you're not here so she takes it all out on me and Da, though he's smart enough to stay out in the fields from sun-up to sundown,' she said slapping the bald bird down and removing the feathers that had stuck to her forearm.

'Where is she?'

Lizzie jerked her head in the direction of the roof. 'Up there, probably counting her cigarette cards.'

'Counting them?'

'She thinks things are disappearing. As if anyone would steal a cigarette card of W. G. Grace.'

I shook my head. 'Da's out in the fields?'

'The bottom field, I think. You going to go see him?'

'Aye. Unless you want a hand.'

'There's no room for two in here, especially when one of them is a lump like you. Go see Da. Here,' she said. 'Take him out a cup of tea.'

She poured two mugs and I set off with them, down over the lawn and past Ma's flower beds, which looked abandoned. Through the open gate in the old stone wall and into the bottom field. The house and most of the land had once been part of the Inverayne House estate, and had been the gardener's home. It had all been sold off when the Southalls had a cash-flow problem and Da bought it. The land was dotted with high granite walls that enclosed the old gardens and greenhouses, but which were now filled with crops or animals. Dod had joked that the pigs behind their five feet thick, fifteen feet high defences were the best protected pigs in the world. I could see Da at the bottom of the hill, digging. The drainage ditch that diverted flood water from the river had collapsed. It was a two man job at least. He straightened up and, leaning on his spade, peered at the figure approaching him.

'That'll be you, Jackie?'

'Aye. Got some tea for you.'

I was suddenly aware that I still had my forage cap on. I wished I could whip the cap off but couldn't without spilling the tea. I reached my father, who eyed me with a sceptical expression. 'Helluva smart. Fit are ye?'

'Leading Aircraftman '

'Ye been up yet?'

'Aye, twelve hours.'

'Solo?'

'Aye.'

'Imagine that. An here's me thinking it's only the likes of yon Southalls that get tae dae thon.'

'Aye, well. There's a war on. Shakes things up a bit.'

'It does that, laddie, right enough.' He drained the lukewarm tea. 'Ye get back the now?'

'Aye, half an hour or so.'

'Well, you'll be well rested.'

I took the hint. 'You needing a hand?'

'No needin but I wouldnae say no.'
'I'll just go change. You got a shovel down here already?'
'No, grab one on your way back.'
'Aye.'

Changing back into my old clothes and getting a spade in my hands. It wasn't another world or another time, it was the same year and these were the same crops I'd helped plant. Definitely fitter though. Even Da commented. The trench needed lengthening, deepening and reinforcing, so we worked from the middle out in opposite directions, digging down and back, away from the river, using the dirt and rocks to build up a bank on the riverside. In spring the river widened and deepened, and in the years before the ditch had been dug the bottom of the field had been a bog. Earthworks and drainage had extended the amount of usable land and kept the river at bay. It needed constant attention. How quickly I'd got out of the rhythms of farm life, working while there was sunlight, resting when it was dark. I kept wondering what time it was, but it didn't matter. What were the lads up to? Not digging, that was sure. Terry would be making some money, selling or buying. Doug would be outside, like me, maybe walking, maybe reading, maybe spending time with his parents.

'No done yet, Dod,' Da called over. 'I'll let you know when we're done.'

I didn't acknowledge the mistake, just got back to work. What brought it on today?

The sun was setting and it was getting harder to see. We'd done a hell of a lot and I even got a pat on the back as we were walking up through the field. 'Good bit of work there. That RAF'll make a man oot e yi yet.'

'So they tell me.'

'They treatin ye richt?'

'Aye. It's hard, ken? But it's hard for everyone.'

'That's good. Sorry aboot that, back there. Cryin ye Dod.'

'Dinnae worry.'

'Jist yer startin tae look affy like him, especially in thon uniform.'

I was surprised he even noticed the mistake, let alone brought it up.

'I think av still got a bottle around somewhere. You'll join me in a dram?'

'Aye, thanks very much.'

We sat around the table while Ma ran in and out of the kitchen, fussing despite the fact that Lizzie had done everything. Lizzie was sitting opposite me wishing Da didn't think it uncivilised for women to drink. Ma had said little to me since we'd returned and washed up for dinner. Nothing more than an 'ah, you're back then?' Since then she'd been pretending to be busy, running about, acting as if she'd just remembered the most important thing, stopping mid-step and turning on the spot. The performance meant ignoring that Lizzie actually did all the work. Eventually, Ma sat down, the food on the table beginning to get cold. Da seemed oblivious, especially after the whisky had been poured. He wasn't much of a drinker – you can't be when you have to get up at dawn and deal with beasts – and his cheeks were already flushed, even though we were only at the soup. The soup was thin and watery, what with rations and the time of year, and I had to admit that so far, mess food was more filling, but whatever herbs Lizzie had used were the exact taste of home. This soup, I now realised, thin though it was, was what I thought of when I thought of home. That smell, that taste. Had Lizzie learned the recipe exactly from Ma? Or had she been cooking it all along?

'So, Jackie,' she said. 'Tell us all about it. You've been gallivanting around the country and your letters contained so little information they could've been written by anyone.'

'It's the censors,' I said. 'We're not allowed to write down any details about our postings in case the enemy gets hold of them. They'd love to know exactly where a few hundred air crew are being trained and stop us ever getting to fly against them.'

Ma coughed, choking almost. 'Well,' said Lizzie. 'There are no spies here, unless Hitler's become so desperate he's recruited Ma.'

'Me? A spy? What a thing to say about your own mother!'

Lizzie rolled her eyes. 'So, where were you?'

I told them about my life since leaving in the spring, about the train to London, living in Abbey Road, the training, eating in the zoo, the postings to Babbacombe, to Cliffe Pypard, about flying. 'The English Riviera, eh? Lounging on the beach while the rest of us were doing the lambing.' She winked at me. 'Not bad for some.'

Soapy, Micky and the others. The red sea. The church. Carrying out those tiny corpses. Clive's kite spread across the runway. 'Were a the creatures still at the zoo?' Da said.

'No. Most have been moved out to the country. The dangerous ones were killed off.'

'Just as well,' said Lizzie.

'Meaning there's a farm aboot the country somewhere wi a great elephant lumbering aroon it?' He chuckled, toasted the idea. It crossed my mind he'd get on with Joe.

'It was nice and warm, but we didnae have much free time,' I said, returning to Lizzie's questions. 'I've been studying harder than I ever did at school.'

'Well, that wouldnae be hard,' said Lizzie. Da was listening, happy with his food, his whisky and his family around, with thoughts of all manner of animals roaming the country. Ma was lost. 'You must have had some fun,' Lizzie said. 'What did you do in London?'

The Windmill. I flirted briefly with the idea of telling them about the real life Titians. Ma would pay attention then, the shock, what would the neighbours say? 'Some fun, aye. I met some guys who like the same music as me, so started a band. Played at a couple of dances.'

'Ach, that's good,' said Da. 'Gettin some use oot o thon bugle.'

The chicken's carcass was stripped bare, the odd strand of dark meat hanging from the skeleton. We sat back, the oily satisfaction of a roast dinner. Ma had hardly touched her food. She was getting thinner. Lizzie began clearing up.

'You'll be comin ben the hoose,' Da said. I nodded and followed him through to the sitting room. Despite the lingering summer heat I wished the fire was going. There was nothing that said 'home' more than a roaring fire in the red brick fireplace, the flames flickering off the brass ornaments on the mantelpiece. The bookcase, the watercolour of the old waterwheel, the dried flower displays Ma did. Lizzie came in and topped up the glasses, then sat beside me.

'So,' Lizzie said. 'What have you got planned while you're here?'

'No much. Just thought I'd help Da out, do whatever needs done. See Willie.'

'A shame, that lad,' Da said.

'He's back home now,' said Lizzie. 'He's... no the happiest of folk these days.'

'I wouldn't have thought so,' I said.

'Aye, I'm not saying he's not entitled but, well, I'm just saying, he's not the same Willie Rennie you'll remember.'

'Aye.'

'When you going back?' Da said.

'A fortnight.'

We finished the ditch. I helped with the crops and the animals, did many of the little jobs that got over-looked: sharpening tools, untangling twine, cleaning out and repairing, all the jobs that seem unimportant in themselves but which would save him a lot of delay and trouble later on. I could switch off my mind and just dig, lift, carry. The satisfying tiredness of a day's work was far superior to the bored exhaustion of a route march. Starting to unwind. I'd never thought that coming home would be a holiday, but when I rejoined the lads in Manchester I'd be ready and refreshed.

I kept meaning to go see Willie, but there was always something to do. Da really needed my help. One morning I glanced at the paper. The headline announced the invasion of Italy. I scanned the article and realised Willie's regiment were involved. Da gave me the day off. Old Rennie and his wife ran the village shop and lived behind it. It was one of those village shops that sold anything. Over the years Old Rennie had amassed the kind of eclectic stock that would satisfy the needs of everyone in Inverayne. As a kid I'd thought the place an Aladdin's cave of wonders. I went through the door, the bell jangling, and wove my way between shelves and around stacks.

'Who's that?' said a voice at the back of the shop.

'It's Jack Devine, Missus Rennie.'

I found her behind the counter with a teapot and a copy

of that day's paper.

'It is Jack Devine,' she said. 'I never recognised you in that get up. Stand straight, let's have a look at you.'

I did. I was unsure how to act. If Willie Rennie had died I'd have known what to do, but he wasn't dead, he was somewhere, in the house presumably, without a leg. What was the correct decorum? I'm sorry for your loss?

'So you're finally a pilot then?' she said.

'No yet, Missus Rennie. I'm still training. Soon though, I hope.'

'It seems to take an affy long time tae learn tae fly,' she said. 'You're nineteen now?'

'I am, aye.' Same age as Willie.

'Have you even been in a plane yet?'

'Aye. I've done twelve hours.'

'Twelve hours? And now you're back on leave?'

'Aye.' I didn't want to go into all the training, to justify myself. I knew from Ma's reaction when Dod died that the question of fairness or not was of paramount importance. Instead I said, 'It's hard to train us here. They need all the planes for fighting.'

'Aye, well,' she said. 'The sooner you get trained the sooner we can win this war. Nae dallying, ye hear?'

'Aye, Missus Rennie.'

'Right, you'll be wanting to see Willie. He's ben the hoose.' She moved slightly to let me through the counter, along the passage and into the house. I pushed my way through into the kitchen and found Old Rennie sitting at the table.

'Hello, Mister Rennie,' I said. 'Missus Rennie said it was okay to come through.'

'Aye,' he said, barely looking up. 'I'm here to see Willie. Is he about?'

'Doon the field playin fitba.'

'Sorry?'

'Far div ye think he is? Ben the hoose drinking tea wi his foot up, the lazy bugger.'

Willie was on the sofa, legs stretched out. One of them must be wooden. The wireless was on, some classical music. 'Hello Willie.'

Willie looked up, surprised. Must've been miles away. 'Jack? Is that you?'

'Aye. Got some leave so came back for a couple of days. Heard you were back and all, so I thought I'd come and see how you're doing.'

'Aye, I'm here. No on leave though. Or permanently on leave. One or the other.'

I didn't know if I should ask about what happened. I decided to stick to safe ground. 'Anything good on?' I said, nodding at the radio.

'Damn all. Never is, not during the day. ITMA's on later.'

'What have you been up to?'

Willie looked at me as if I was soft. 'What do you think? Playin fitba?'

'Your Da already made that joke.'

A pause, then Willie laughed. 'Miserable bastard, too cheap to even think up his ain jokes, now he's stealin mine.' His laughter seemed to break something in the room. 'I've no been doin anything much, Jack. They gave me thon things tae get aroon on,' he gestured at the crutches leaning against the wall. 'But whits the point? Where the hell am I gonnae go in this place?'

'Aye, suppose.'

'So how's life in the RAF? All those mechanics. You should've joined the Army, Jack.'

'What, and miss out on this pilot's uniform? No chance.'

'Aye, the birds do love it, that's true. You get any of that down south?'

'No really, you know what it's like. Never a minute in the forces.'

'Aye, I ken exactly fit it's like. Spare minute and every man is straight doon the hoorhoose before you can say "payday". Dinnae play the innocent wi me.'

'No kidding. We tried the one time, in London, but the place had been bombed out.'

'Nae luck. Still, you'll have tae get it out the wrapper soon. You dinnae want tae die a virgin, do you?'

I tried to control myself. 'Whit are ye thinking?' said Willie. 'Are ye thinking "shame a cannae tell a cripple tae get tae fuck"?'

'No,' I said. 'I was just wondering if, since you'd got back, you'd managed to get your log over?'

For a second I thought I'd gone too far, but Willie burst out laughing, a high, hard laugh that sounded like it'd been dying to come out for ages. 'For Christ's sake Jack, that's a good one. Get your log over? Oh, am stealing that yin.' I looked around the dark, musty room, and at the tiredness on Willie's face. The clock said five past eleven.

'Come on,' I said. 'We're aff oot.'

'Am no going anywhere.'

'Aye you are, and I'm no asking. The Clansman opened five minutes ago and I'm buying.'

Willie looked like he was going to argue, but I just handed him his crutches.

'Now, either use those things or I'm going to carry you there like you really were a cripple.'

Willie pulled himself up shakily, leaning on the crutches like a new born calf. We moved slowly through to the kitchen.

'I'm just taking Willie out to get legless, Mister Rennie,' I said on the way by. 'Aye,' he said, turning a page in the paper.

The pub was empty. Everyone was off fighting, working, contributing somehow. I ordered two pints, taking comfort in the uniform. 'So what's it like,' he said, 'the flying?'

'Nothing like it. Up there alone, just you and the kite.'

'And Jerry.'

'Aye. Well, no yet. But it'll come.'

'Still got the training wheels on you?'

'For a while. We're getting shipped overseas for more training.'

'Overseas?'

'Canada, South Africa, Rhodesia, somewhere like that.'

'Far from the fighting.'

'They need the kites here for fighting.'

'Still. It's no all training, Jack. There's fighting to be done.'

'Hey, don't tell me about fighting. I've suffered. Back in London, three whole weeks and no clean sheets. And they only let us have seconds at dinner. No more than that.'

'Get tae fuck.'

Another round. 'You make any mates?'

'Aye, a couple. Started a band.'

'Aye? Some war you're having.'

'Leave it, eh? Tell me this, you've been in a while. You had any grief?'

'Apart from the leg?'

'Aye, I mean, I've a… well, yeah, a mate, and he's big on the Scotland against England stuff. And Dod got a lot of stick for his accent. You had anything?'

'No more than anyone else.'

'This mate, he thinks we're different. Should be a different country. As much for fighting the English as for fighting the Germans.'

'Well dinnae listen tae him, Jack. Forget him. Think about your own experiences. You feel like a foreigner down there?'

'No, not really.'

'Well then. Dinnae worry about banter, all the "jock" stuff. It's no about us, it's just lads being lads. We dinnae get it anymore than anyone else, and we all gie it out. You remember at school? We all had nicknames, we all got the piss ripped out of us. At the end of they day, we're all still mates. Your mates are your mates. End of.'

'Aye, I suppose.'

'Listen, if they really think you're a cunt, you'll know it. We had one boy in my unit, one boy everyone hated. People did stuff tae him all the time, pissed on his bed, put things in his grub, sent him tae dae all the suicide missions, laying cables during mortar fire, things like that.'

'Why did everyone hate him?'

'Never did work that out. Just something about him.'

'He still out there?'

'Nope. Hanged himself.'

'That's horrible.'

'Aye. I'm empty.'

Another round. Another. I wondered if Willie knew about Italy. Another round. I came back from the toilet. He'd the paper open.

'Fucking useless, I am,' he said. 'Sitting here when I should be shooting Itis with the lads.'

'Lot of use you'd be in a beach landing,' I said. 'Long John Silver sinking into the sand.'

'I could be amphibious,' he said. 'Float across from Salerno.'

'Wouldn't work. Your leg would float to the top, flipping you upside down.'

'I knew this thing would be the death of me.'

Gallows humour, the only way to cope. Distraction. Get him thinking about something else. 'That lad I was telling you about. The one who hates the English.'

I told him about Joe. 'Sounds like he did it, aye,' said Willie.

'What should I do?'

'What dae you mean "what should I do?"'

'I mean, should I say anything. Should I turn him in?'

'Turn him in? Grass him up? Are you fucking kidding me? He's a mate?'

'He was, aye.'

'Doesnae matter. You dinnae grass up anyone, mate or no. You know that, Jack. You're no a cunt.'

'But if he murdered him?'

'Then he'll get his one day. There's a war on. People dying every day. I honestly cannae find it in me tae give much of a fuck, Jack. I really can't.'

'You don't think I've a duty?'

'To who? Since when were you William Wallace? It's no your job tae bring justice tae this world, Jack. It's your job tae stand by your mates, dae your best and, if need be, die for your country. Anything else is just shite. Empty.'

Another round in, and another. When the pub closed for the afternoon I took Willie home, laying him out on the sofa where I'd first found him. Mrs Rennie didn't look too happy at drinking during the day, but seemed that really was the first time Willie had been out the house for weeks. The one balanced the other. Da took one look at me and told me to sleep it off.

I climbed the stairs. I lay back, my old room. Dod's room.

Dod's bed was still there, as were his pictures, his books, his clothes. Ma wouldn't have anything touched. When Dod first left I couldn't sleep. The room was wrong, an emptiness. Slowly I got accustomed to the emptiness, but it never felt right. Now I'd been away it was even less like my own. I lay back on the bed and looked at the model planes hanging from the roof. The Tiger Moth was inaccurate. The ones I'd flown had no tail wheel, just a skid. My model had a wheel. I leaned over and switched on the record player, Louis Armstrong. How many times had I fallen asleep listening to Satchmo blow beautiful? Dod's empty bed. Willie's wooden leg. What would happen to me? Sleep came then, the fast, deep, dreamless sleep after daytime drinking. I didn't wake until the sun had set and dinner was served. Da seemed to understand the mercy mission I'd been on, but he didn't offer me any whisky that night.

More work. Digging, lifting, building. Alone in the big field with my trumpet. The sound, the lone brass blast, wasn't enough anymore. The solitary notes were hollow without Terry's piano, Joe's drums. Back against the trunk, trumpet at my side, eyes closed, hoping for emptiness, hoping for answers.

Dod. All those lads in Babbacombe. Clive. Willie's leg. Could be my turn any day.

Makes you think.

Straighten up and fly right, Jack.

Sunday came round. I packed my kit.

Next morning. Ma cried. Da saw me off at the end of the road. Lizzie walked me to the station. I chapped on Willie's window, gave him a wave. Didn't stop. A second leaving. This time I knew what was waiting for me.

I thought I'd meet him. I'd no idea how many trains went from Glasgow to Manchester every day, but Joe was always going to be on mine. He crashed down, breath strong with beer. Nothing I could do. Couldn't tell him to fuck off. I offered him a fag, lit his, lit mine. 'Good holiday?' he said.

'Aye. You?'

'Shite. No-one's around, no-one tae have fun with. City full of women, weans and old yins. Same in Teuchterland?'

'Aye. One pal was home, leg blown off.'

I looked at him. Still no idea what to do. Willie said you stand by your pals no matter what. A mate's a mate. End of.

'Any idea how long we're in Manchester?' he said.

'No. It's an Air Crew Despatch Centre, so I guess we're there until they despatch us.'

'Overseas, eh? Sun, flying and dusky maidens. Where dae you think we'll go?'

'No idea.'

'I know that, you're no fucking Bomber Harris, but you must have thoughts.'

Too many. 'America would be nice.'

'Jazz.'

'Jazz.'

'Hey,' said Joe, 'if we're in Manchester more than a couple of days, we should see about getting the band back together.'

And have you behind me, where I can't see you? 'Doubt Terry will be up for it.'

'Like a bloody woman, that one. Mood swings, silent treatment. Hopefully a fortnight in the valleys will have sorted him out. Couple of turns with an experienced sheep and he'll be right as rain. Any idea what was wrong with him, anyway?'

'What?' Was he being serious?

'He was acting like every day was his time of the month. Nearly had tae give him a slap a couple of times.'

What was wrong with him? 'He was angry with you, Joe.'

'With me? Why?'

'Over the whole Clive business.'

'That wasnae the problem. That was the, what's it called? The symptom.'

I had no idea what he was going on about. 'Joe, that thing with Clive, that affected us all. We were all caught up in it. And then with how it ended up—'

'That was a fucking accident, Jack,' he said leaning over and stabbing me with his finger.

'Aye, fine, but you have to realise not everyone has the same attitude to violence as you do.'

'I know that,' he said. 'There are babies everywhere, frightened by a little blood, scared of a little pain. I'm looking at one now. But that's no Terry. He's no a fucking milksop like you, Jack. He couldn't give a damn about Clive. If he's cheesed off at me and no just taking it out on me, then it's for something other than giving Clive what he deserved.'

Heaton Park, Manchester. September – October 1943

Air Crew Despatch Centre, Heaton Park, Manchester. One big outdoor waiting room. Acres and acres of Absolutely Nothing. Heaton Park had been a family estate that put Inverayne House to shame. Rolling hills, ponds, open spaces and tree cover. A bit of everything: An enclosed world. The original house sprawled, enormous wings of columns either side of the main building. Comrade Joe was soon lecturing about the outrage, reclamation of land, redistribution of wealth. Well, it had been redistributed. From the aristocracy to the military. Hills, trees and ponds; quite idyllic really, all that nature. Would've been quite pleasant if it hadn't been full of bored servicemen.

All we had to do was wait for our postings. We thought it would be a day or two, a week at the most. The first night as we sat outside our tents smoking, Doug got talking to another Yorkshire lad, Tom. 'I've been here four weeks and not a peep about orders. Get settled in, boys. You could be here til Christmas.'

Of course, there were training exercises, guard duty, even the odd go on a rifle range but usually after fatigues and parade there was nothing to do. We'd walk across the park, round the perimeter, circle the ponds and lakes, up the hills, down again. Trudging on. Slowstepping. If we were lucky we could make it last all day. I had nothing to do but think. My mind scattered from one subject to another. I took to doing push ups and sit ups, trying to use the energy, exhaust my mind. Technically, we were prisoners. No-one was allowed out without a pass. Some of the lads were billeted in the local community, and for a fee they'd give up their passes for a night. Others tried going over the wall. Terry quickly got to know Stella in the office and in return for luxuries she'd stamp blank passes for him. By the third night he'd got two blanks and Tom gave his pass to Doug. The three of us could hit the town. We were on a countdown and the chances of us all being posted together were tiny. At a stretch Terry and I, purely as a result of our last names, might end up on the same boat, but we really had no idea how they decided these things. Every night could be our last together.

'So, where are we going?' I asked Terry. Joe was on guard duty.

'Stella says there's a decent place about ten minutes from here.'

'Pub?'

'Pub. Take your trumpet.'

'Why?'

'Why? Because we might need a spittoon. So you can play it of course.'

'Do you know anywhere we can play?'

'Stella says they have music in there sometimes. Lots of Yanks drink there.'

We got by the guards no problem, our forged passes

standing up to the casual glance, and found the pub easily enough. It was empty, a handful of locals, some Yanks, British uniforms. Terry had his bag of goods with him. We sank a couple of beers, the first hardly touching the sides. There was a piano, but Terry didn't seem inclined to play. He seemed to be examining the place, his searching, evaluating look going over each customer and the landlord. I nodded at the piano. 'Fancy a jam?'

'Yes, but hold on, I've got some business to attend to first.'

'Sales?'

'Potentially.'

I got another round in. Terry hardly spoke, seemed to be waiting for something. Doug and I swapped stories about our leave, but I didn't really want to talk about it. Three pints down the door opened and a tall, thin man in civilian clothes came in. As soon as he saw him, Terry went up to the bar. They shook hands, got drinks and sat down at a different table. 'Are you all right, Jack?'

'Why?'

'Since you came back from leave you've been different.'

'Different?'

'You're drinking more.'

I shrugged. 'Fuck all else to do.'

'So,' said Doug. 'Is the band a duo now?'

'I suppose so. Terry and Joe hate each other.'

'And you?'

'I don't know. What Joe did to Clive, I don't think I can forgive that.'

'They got even though. Clive got him with the bottle. Or are you talking about something else?' My drink was empty, Doug had hardly touched his. I got myself another. The bar in Soho. Smiled a bit at the memory. All that had happened since then. But Joe had ruined it all. Prick. He should be there, the four of us drinking, playing music. There'd be an ENSA show soon in some local theatre, we could've played in it, but I was beginning to wish that the postings would come through and we'd be off. The drink was going to my head. Terry came back. 'You work fast, don't you?' I said.

'That's business. If you don't move fast, you're dead.'

'What you selling?'

'The usual. Whatever people want to buy.' He looked at us, sensed the atmosphere. 'Problem?'

'Jack's got something on his mind,' said Doug.

'Sharing?' said Terry.

Fuck it. So I told them about Joe, about the night before Clive's crash, seeing Joe under one of the kites. 'I knew it,' said Terry. 'I fucking knew it.'

'You're sure?' said Doug. 'Sure he wasn't just pissing?'

'No,' I said. 'It's not like I caught him with a pair of pliers and his hands in the engine. But…'

'But what?'

'Just his attitude. And you both saw him after the crash. He didn't seem surprised.'

'Proof,' said Doug. 'You've got no proof.'

'We can't say anything,' I said. Doug shook his head.

'We can't not say anything,' said Terry.

'To who?' I said. 'Maybe if I'd said something to Thor, he might have believed us, but here, in Manchester? No-one knows us, or him. The RAF put it down as accidental death. Who's going to believe us? Who's going to give a fuck?'

'Fine, but we can't let him get away with it.'

'So what?'

'Revenge,' said Terry. 'You don't mean…'

'No, don't be daft. Look, let me have a think about it, but I might have an idea.'

'You need to be sure,' said Doug. 'If you're going to do something serious, this level of serious, then you need to be sure.'

'Are you sure, Jack?'

I thought about it, Joe, his actions, his reactions. 'Aye, he did it.'

'And you're prepared to do something about that? This isn't something you can change your mind about later,' said Terry.

Drink. 'Aye, I'm in. You can't let people get away with things like that.' Take action, Jack. Do something. This is something. 'Fine. Now, let's change the mood here. Some music?' Aye. Lose myself.

Joe's tent was next to mine and as far as he was concerned we were still friends. I tried to be as cold with him as I could, but he either didn't notice or didn't care. Too much free time. I was cooking. I needed an outlet, a release. I took my trumpet to a quiet part of the park, played like it was the field at home. Musical shelter. Escape.

We were called into the big hut and issued with new kit. Took it back to our tents, dumped it in a pile. 'Shorts?' said Terry.

'Rhodesia then,' said Doug. Rhodesia. What to make of that? A bit of an anti-climax. Smoke drifted from three cigarettes as we mulled.

'Must be soon if they're giving us the kit,' I said. 'How long does the boat to Rhodesia take?'

No-one knew. 'Can we get a pint in Rhodesia?' asked Terry. 'I heard some countries out that way are dry. Muslim and that.'

No-one knew. 'A pal of mine was in Africa,' I said. 'In

the north.'

'Isn't Rhodesia in the south?' said Doug.

No-one was sure. 'Some bad fighting in North Africa,' said Terry. 'A few mates from back home were out that way. Hotter than buggery, sand and insects and things that like to bite. Mate of mine is in the tanks. Imagine being in one of those tin contraptions in that heat. Squashed like a sardine then baked.'

A 'Brew Up' they called it. Willie told me. When a tank was hit and a fire broke out inside. Became like an oven. Like a kettle. Everyone inside got cooked. A brew up. You had to laugh. 'So. Rhodesia, eh?' Terry said.

'Aye.'

'Rhodesia.'

'You got any more to offer than that?'

'Just saying, you know? Rhodesia.'

Joe turned up, flung his new kit in his tent. 'No gonnae be much action there as far as I can see. Don't know about you boys but I signed up tae kill some Fascists, no sit in some fucking desert miles from the action playing with myself. Christ, why can we no just get on with it? Sitting around here with our thumbs up our arses waiting tae be shipped off tae bloody Nowhereland. I want tae be killing Fascists no smoking in Manchester or smoking in Rhodesia. At this rate the war'll be over and we'll still be sitting here, smoking.'

No-one answered him. 'Hey, Jack,' said Terry, 'I got a couple of passes. Up for it?'

'Fuck yes,' I said. 'I need to get out of here.'

Joe looked at us. Waited for his invite. Nothing.

'So, it's like that, is it?' he said. We said nothing. He left.

Same pub, another sale, another jam. A few other RAF lads, over the wall or forged passes, same as us. During one of

Terry's compositions, the pub door opened and in walked three black GIs. One went to the bar and ordered drinks, the other two made straight for us. Terry, who had his back to the door, didn't see them. The atmosphere in the pub shifted. I was reminded of the fight in the London club. There'd been a lot of sounding off in the papers recently about black Yanks courting British women, and often producing mixed race babies. Some muttering ran through the pub, but no-one had the balls, or was drunk enough to say anything. One of the GIs leaned on the piano.

'Hey man, that's great playing.'

'Thanks,' said Terry. I stopped playing, but Terry continued.

'Yeah,' said the other. 'We were walking past and we heard. Had to come in. We play here too sometimes.'

'You can play?' said Terry.

'Can we play? Course we can play. We're from New Orleans. In New Orleans if you don't play, you ain't nothin'.'

The third man came over with the drinks. 'Hey,' he said. 'George is the name.' He put the drinks down and shook hands. 'Jack, Terry, this is Nathanial and Jed.'

'New Orleans,' I said. 'Really?'

Nathanial nodded. 'Yeah, really. Hey, do you mind?'

I hesitated, but handed it over. The sounds he got out of it. Incredible. He played like the band in London, that new sound. 'What is that?' I said to George. 'That style of jazz.'

'You like?'

'I heard it once in London, couldn't forget it.'

'That's what they're calling bebop. It's the next thing, but it hasn't made it here yet. I mean, here it's still all swing and big band.'

'Who's doing this?' I said. 'Are there any records I can listen to?'

'You ever heard of Dizzy Gillespie?'

'I know him,' I said. 'He was in Cab Calloway's band.'

'That's the fella,' said George. 'Well, you should hear what he's doing now. It's the future, baby. Guys like Dizzy and Charlie Parker.'

Nathanial finished, took a drink.

'That was great,' I said. 'You think you could teach me?'

'Why not?' said Nathanial. 'Say, you guys like a party?'

'What do you mean?'

'We were just on our way to one. You come with us, we can jam some there.'

I looked at the time. 'We need to be back by midnight.'

'You turn into a pumpkin?'

'Rules.'

I looked at Terry. He shrugged. 'More ways into the park than just the gates.' Did I really want to turn down this chance? Don't sit waiting for something to happen, Jack. Make it happen.

'Fuck it,' I said. 'Why not?'

We followed them down the street. Row after row of identical houses, blackouts up, gaps like missing teeth, rubble neatly contained within a lot. Whispering lest noise carry, curtains twitch, RAF issue boots outrageously loud on the pavements. Didn't want to meet some ARP, MP, explain ourselves. The streets were deserted. Ghost town. A low rumbling crossed the border of our hearing. Four years of war had ingrained that sound. Bombers. We had control of the skies, raids were becoming rarer. No need to panic, but it wasn't a good idea to be out in the streets. The bombers passed over and the fighters went up to meet them. We stopped walking, watched the darting Spitfires and Hurricanes, desperate for the day we could join them in the sky. Now we'd gone solo, had spent some time in an aircraft, we watched the show with more intelligent eyes. Neither of us had been inside a proper fighter but we'd studied them enough. I mentally went through the movements, the combined action of arms, legs, the sweep of the head, the calculations that went into each roll, dive and shot. A fraction of the adrenaline the pilots up there were feeling, but I understood enough to recognise the metallic taste. A Junkers took the final fiery dive. Cheer. When a Hurricane took a hit and the pilot bailed out we felt the sickness of fear. This would happen to us one day. Would I be lucky enough to bail out? Returning bombers passed overhead. One of them was slower than the others, limping at the back, smoke. Then we heard it, that whistle. We all knew that whistle. 'Fuck!'

Dived into the nearest garden and ducked behind the wall. The blast rocked us, dust and smoke everywhere, ringing, a loud persistent ringing. Picking ourselves up, dazed. A bomb had landed on the house three doors down. No chance. Whoever was in there was a goner. Terry recovered his wits quickest.

'Now would be a good time to leave,' he said.

'Maybe we can help.' I thought of the church and felt sick. The fire brigade would be on the scene soon enough, and we didn't want to be around when they did. We tore ourselves away from the burning remains.

'Maybe we should go back,' said Terry.

'We're going on,' said Nathanial. I looked at them, at Terry.

The party was in a house shared by three nurses the Yanks were seeing. The girls were hesitant at first to let us strangers in but eventually relented when Terry produced a bottle of whisky. The near miss woke us all up, filled us with energy. They talked but I wanted to get to it. Nathanial saw that, got his trumpet out, and I got mine, and he set about teaching me some bebop. The fast tempo I'd already got from listening in London, but the harmonic structures, the asymmetrical phrasing, that's what I'd noticed and didn't know how to replicate. 'See, man,' he said, 'Satchmo would go from here to here, take the next step, maybe mute it. Now Charlie Parker, he'd have none of that. He'd go to the flat ninth, maybe, improv from the higher intervals of the chord.'

He showed me phrases, and I copied, learned to relax into the freedom. 'The trick's fighting your muscles, letting your instinct take over, letting what you hear in your head, letting that come through your fingers.'

I could feel it, tingling, something coming through me and out the trumpet. Wrapped in it, afloat in it, could feel my fingers hurting, the speed new, but I couldn't stop, a new world, set foot in a new world. 'Try this out. This is Dizzy.' He played a piece, slow at first, swinging, high notes tinged with melancholy. The vibrato Nathanial could pull off.

'What's that?'

'Called *Night in Tunisia*.'

I thought of Willie, his leg in the desert. 'Show me again.'

Terry tapped me on the shoulder. 'We'd better get going, Jack. It'll be light soon.' The girls had gone to bed, as had George and Jed. He'd just been listening. I hadn't noticed. I wanted to stay there forever playing bebop, learning, improving, growing, but Terry was right.

'You guys drink there a lot?' said Nathanial.

'When we can get passes,' said Terry.

'See you in there sometime.'

'Definitely.'

We only just made it before sunrise. I boosted Terry onto the wall, he pulled me up, dropped into some bushes. Laughing, we got back to our tents. 'You look happy, Jack,' Terry said.

'Man,' I said. 'That was a fun night.'

'Good. I'll get some more passes.'

'And how about...' I paused. It seemed wrong but I couldn't ignore the urge. The energy from the music, the bomb, the frustrations. 'How about some fun?' I said

'Fun?'

'You know, the kind of fun you had in Soho.'

'You serious?'

Exhausted, only an hour of sleep before parade, but the glow in me, the stretched, warm lungs. Please let them ship me to America. We were told to return the kit we'd been given. Apparently they did this quite often in case there were any spies in the camp. Everyone gets shorts so the spy sends off a message saying 'pilots off to Africa' then they recall the shorts and give us snow gear, or something like that. Causes confusion in the enemy and hopefully the spy pisses off his superiors and they put him up against the wall. I thought this was applying logic after the fact, attempting to explain the inexplicable.

'So what the fuck is all this then?' said Joe.

We were outside our tents, smoking, the sun setting. It'd been three days since Terry and I went out. I had my trumpet out practicing what Nathanial had taught me. Any spare moment now, I played. People told me to shut up, but I ignored them. This was what I wanted to be doing. They'd be gone soon, or I would. I could stand their insults until then.

'All what?'

'All this? How have you suddenly learned a totally new style of jazz?'

'A mate taught me it.'

'A mate? Apart from me, Taffy and Doug, you havenae got any mates.'

'Aye, Joe. That's right.'

'It is right.'

'Fuck off.'

'So what's going on?'

'Terry and I met some Yanks, one of them taught me the basics of bebop.'

'This in that bar?'

'Aye.'

'So youse two are going out playing jazz and it didnae occur tae you tae invite your drummer?'

'Our drummer? The band's over, Joe. We haven't played together since Babbacombe.'

'Aye, only because we havenae got a drum kit.'

'No.'

'Oh, is that it? Well, fuck me, now I've seen everything. You've gone and picked Terry over me. Taken fucking sides.'

'I'm not taking sides, Joe.'

'Aye, you are.'

'Joe against the world. Seconds out, round two.' I hadn't seen Terry approach.

'Fuck you, Taffy.'

'Joe. I'm not scared of you, okay?'

'You'd better watch.'

'What are you going to do? Rifle butt in the back of the head? Or are you going to follow me overseas and fiddle with my kite?'

I thought Joe would go for him, but he didn't move. Instead he just stared at me. 'So, you told him, did you?

Thought I could trust you, Jack. Another Scot. No loyalty then, have you?'

'Loyalty? That's fucking rich, Joe.'

'Aye, is it? Well, you'd better watch and all.'

He flicked his fag at my face, walked off. 'We'd better step this up,' said Terry. 'We could be posted any day and now he knows, he could do anything.'

'But what are we going to do?'

'It's all worked out.'

'What is?'

'Simple. He can't be nicked for one crime, so we just make sure he's nicked for another.'

'Frame him?'

'Like a watercolour.'

Get involved, Jack.

A few nights later we got out again, back to the bar, met up with the Yanks. I'd been practicing hard and it paid off. We jammed for hours. I didn't drink more than a pint, just using it to wet my lips. This was it, the stuff I'd been looking for. The band, the groove, I never wanted to leave that bar. Joe had been right after all. My first band was special, but it wasn't the best.

I still wanted to hear some bebop, see what else was there, what Nathanial hadn't taught me, what I could find for myself, but there were no records in Britain and nothing on the wireless. America, please, America. After, Terry took me to one side. 'Are you still up for it?'

'Aye.'

'And you've got the money?'

'Aye.'

'Come on then.'

'Now remember, this is a business transaction. This is not romantic. This is not love. She does not love you, she's paid to pretend. It's no different than going to a restaurant. You order off the menu and if you don't get what you ordered, you complain. Right?'

'Aye.'

Up three flights of stairs. The place was a firetrap, wall hangings, candles, scarves and weird Eastern decorations hanging from the ceiling. Five pints in me, ready for this. Strangely, I couldn't help thinking of the jazz club in London. It had the same feel, some atmosphere. To think of it like jazz made it familiar. Five girls. Low light. 'You have to choose one, Jack.'

'His first time?'

'It is.'

'Take Shirley, she'll be gentle with him.'

I looked at Shirley. She looked like one of the girls in The Windmill, like she'd been in my year at school. Not that. I didn't want that. 'No. I want that one. Sorry, I don't know your name.'

She was black. I hadn't planned it. Maybe it was the jazz. The exotic. Jazz, black music, America. 'Kay?'

I felt bad turning down the first girl, but she just shrugged. Business, I reminded myself. Just business. Kay led me through a curtain. Terry was behind me with his choice. We went into one room, they went into another. He slapped me on the back as he went by.

The room was tiny, a mattress, a seat and a candle burning on tiny table. In the darkness I could hardly see Kay, her skin so black. There was a smell in the room, stale. No window, just the flickering fire. We could still hear the music, the trumpet blowing soft and sad. That world, jazz. Exotic. America. Africa. 'Do you like jazz?' I said.

'Do you?'

'It's beautiful.' When I looked at her I thought of jazz. America. Smoke.

Dancing. She slipped out of her thin dressing gown, stood naked before me. Jazz.

New Orleans.

Black music.

Slave music. She put a finger against my lips, started to undress me. I reached out, tentatively ran a hand over her breast. My cock hard. She stroked a finger along it, guided me down onto the bed.

The candle flame. The smell.

No windows. Jazz.

Black music. Black skin. Slave music. I left. I left alone, out before Terry was done. Waited for him outside. I hadn't done it. Couldn't. That thought. That room. That music. Like Terry said, it's all just business. Willie was wrong. Duty. Right and wrong. Maybe he didn't give a fuck anymore, but I still did.

When we got near the gates, Terry stopped me. Pulled me behind a tree.

'Watch.'

The guards were examining every pass carefully, something they never did.

'I thought he'd do this,' said Terry.

'What?'

'Joe. He's grassed on us. We'd better go over the wall.'

It was almost over, and we knew it. Countdown. Doug was the first to leave. A group were taken off and given their aircrew categorisation. Doug was made a navigator. He was gutted. We all were. They gave him the Rhodesia kit back.

Joe letting on about the forged passes meant it was all but impossible to get out the park, so we couldn't have a decent farewell party for Doug but Terry still managed to produce some whisky. We sat drinking until four in the morning, when he had to make his unsteady way to the station. We shook hands, tight.

'Take care, Doug. Write to me, let me know what Rhodesia's like.'

'Will do, Jack. And after the war…'

'After the war…'

I was really sad to see him go. He was the only one in our group that had never been any trouble.

'It's tomorrow,' said Terry.

'What is?'

'Operation Get Even.'

'You still haven't told me what we're doing.'

'Safer that way. But I'll need your help. Joe's on guard duty tonight and I need to smuggle some stuff into the camp.'

'How are you going to manage that? We can't get passes.'

'I'll go over the wall. It's easy enough, I've been doing it most nights.'

'You go out every night?'

'Most nights.'

There was so much about Terry I didn't know. 'What do you need me to do?'

'I want you to be on this side of the wall at one in the morning. I'm going to chuck some stuff over. I need you there to make sure it's clear before I do. Right?'

'Aye, all right.'

Shortly before one I made my way to the spot below the wall. It was a cold, wet night, and I was shivering by the time

I heard Terry call.

'All clear.'

A canvas kit bag landed about a metre from me. Another one followed. Then Terry came over.

'Quick, grab a bag, get back to the tents.'

We got back without being caught, although we both slipped in the mud. I laughed a little, nervous. We looked camouflaged, perfect for secret work.

'So, what do we do with these?'

'In Joe's tent.'

'In his tent?'

'Yes, under his kit bags, squash them as much as you can so the pile looks the same size.'

'Won't he notice?'

'He's on duty. He won't have time.'

We cleaned up, got back into our tents. Awoken by a shout. Snap inspection. Bleary, we lined up.

'What's going on?' I whispered to Terry.

'Snap inspection.'

'Obviously. Why?'

'Someone believes stolen US Air Force property is being hidden in the park.'

'Why do they believe that?'

'Because someone told them it was.'

'Terry?'

'Eye for an eye, Jack.'

It was inevitable. I watched it unfold with growing nausea. They pulled the kit bags out of Joe's tent. He was still on guard duty. We were dismissed. 'Where's the whisky?' I asked Terry.

'Why?'

'Because I need a fucking drink.'

'To celebrate?'

I said nothing. He handed me a three quarters full bottle.
'Are you on duty today?'

'No.'

'I'll cover you at parade.'

I nodded, grabbed my trumpet and walked off.

A big park. Thank fuck for that, eh? Always somewhere to
hide, somewhere where others aren't there. Lots of places
like that. Where others aren't. Home. Others aren't there.
Dod isn't there. I'm not there. But I'm here. Dod isn't
anywhere. And Doug isn't here. Now Joe isn't here. Clive
isn't here, Micky isn't here, Soapy, Nev. They aren't here.
Am I?

Up in the sky, just wood and canvas, a tent between me and
the ground. Emptiness, nothingness. I can fly. I can fly.

I can see my house from here.

The bottle's empty. Typical.

Straightenupandflyright Straightenupandflyright
Straightenupandflyright, right?

It was done. Joe was gone. His tent empty. I crawled into
mine and passed out.

I sat on the log Joe had used as a seat, smoking. Terry sat
across from me.

'You regret it?'

'Of course.'

'Why?'

'What's the punishment for stealing military stores?'

'No idea.'

'It's harsh?'

'It's harsh. What's the punishment for murder?'

'That's not the point.'

'What is the point, Jack?'

'I don't know. He was a mate.'

'Was he?'

'Once.'

'Look, I told you back in London he was trouble. If you stay too close to someone like him, you get burnt too.'

'Yes, very prescient. Well done. You got burnt as well.'

'Did I?'

'You got involved.'

'Is that the same?'

'You're not sorry?'

'No.'

'Why not?'

'A number of reasons.'

'Humour me.'

'One, he had it coming. He killed Clive by fucking with a kite. That could've been any one of us up there, Jack, you realise that? He didn't know for sure Clive would be up first, and in that kite.'

'Two?'

'Two, the politicos, they're a menace, I told you that too, Jack.'

'His politics? You set him up because he was a Communist?'

'We set him up, and no, not because he was a Communist, but it was his politics that made him dangerous.'

'Joe was right.'

'What?'

'He said this, that your hatred had nothing to do with Clive, that you didn't give a fuck about Clive.'

'I didn't give a fuck about Clive. It's the principle of the thing.'

'The principle? What aren't you telling me? Why do you hate Joe if not because of Clive?'

He sighed, lit another fag. 'I have a brother.'

'You told me, down the mine.'

'Another. He's in prison.'

'In prison? What for?'

Terry looked around, no-one was near. 'He's a conscientious objector.'

'Religious?'

'Political. He's a Communist. At the outbreak of war Stalin and Hitler had that non-aggression pact. In thirty-nine the Communists were opposed to the war, called it a war of Imperialism. Owen refused to fight. Went to prison.'

'But Joe's fighting. Other Communists are fighting.'

'Once Hitler invaded the Soviet Union, it was fine to support the war. Too late for Owen.'

'So what's this got to do with Joe?'

'Have you any idea what it's like having a brother in prison as a conchie?'

'So what, you're getting back at your brother through Joe?'

'Jack, did Joe murder Aircraftman Second Class Clive Wellesley or not?'

'He did.' I hadn't even known Clive's last name.

'And was he going to get away with that?'

'He was.'

'A murder was committed, the murderer is going to jail. What's your problem?'

What was my problem? 'It feels shitty, Terry. To do that

to someone, to fit them up for something. We were trying to get justice, Terry. That's not justice. It's not fair.'

'Justice isn't about being fair, Jack. It's about getting even. One life for another. That's all this war is, Jack, getting even. They bomb London, we bomb Berlin. They flatten Coventry, we flatten Frankfurt. It's not fair, it's not anything, Jack. It's just what there is. Does it feel shitty? Sure, but so does everything else these days.'

The days passed with little change. Rain fell and we huddled under whatever shelter we could find, gas capes as umbrellas failing to keep us dry. We listened to the news every night, passed round papers until they were so faded you could hardly read a word. There were no more passes, no more sneaking out. Security had been stepped up. The jam sessions were over. I was back to playing by myself, alone in a field. Terry and I were civil, but no longer close. I thought I understood him better, but you never could tell with him. Maybe it was for the best, but I couldn't help wishing we were all back in Babbacombe, mates, band mates, strutting down the street looking for women, playing cards in the tall grass, jamming.

Finally, after five weeks, about thirty of us were marched out of the park and into the local cinema. Baffled, we exchanged theories about what was going to happen. Terry wasn't with us. 'Are they actually showing a picture?'

'It'll be some sort of educational thing.'

After twenty minutes or so an officer climbed onto the stage.

'Shit. This is it. Aircrew categorisation time.'

Silence in the cinema.

The officer read out names and their categorisation.

Aitken, F; Navigator. Anderson, J; Pilot. Caldwell, S; Bomb Aimer. Clark, P. T.; Bomb Aimer. Devine, J; Pilot.

Those who got what they wanted attempted to commiserate with friends not so lucky, but few got the tone right. Today's friends wouldn't be there tomorrow. I had no friends there. We trooped back to the park to pack. We were off.

'Congratulations,' said Terry. He looked like he meant it. 'You'll get your orders soon enough.'

'Hope so, there's no-one left to have any fun with.'

'You can always find fun.'

'True. But it won't be the same without you, Jack.'

Did he mean that? 'Maybe after the war…'

'After the war…'

We shook hands. 'Jack,' he said. 'All of this… forget it, right? We're at war. Don't let it fuck up your future. Joe isn't worth that.'

At zero four-thirty hours, far from our best, we assembled and marched over to the train station. The usual panic and crush as seats were fought for and luggage stowed. I couldn't be bothered to fight, ended up in the doorway. Head against the wall. Where was I going?

Honour, duty, Henry the Fifth.

Morning in Cumbria.

Wrongs upon wrongs. Is that what we were fighting for?
Crossed the border somewhere. Home.

You stand by your mates.

Into Glasgow. Off the train. Onto another. All those
voices, accents.

Joe.

Moving again, to the coast.

Straighten up and fly right, Jack.

End of the line. Six of us tasked with the kit, overseen by
a Warrant Officer. I didn't know them. Everyone else onto
the boats. We swung bags, emptied the train, filled a launch.

Salt in the air. Memories.

Loaded.

Decision time.

'Sir, could I speak to you for a moment? It's very important.'

RMS Queen Elizabeth, Atlantic Ocean. October 1943

A wild ocean at night. Mountainous waves, wind like a brick wall, sharp salt whip. How religion takes hold. Early man, huddled in caves along the coast wielding stone axes, flint knives to protect himself from the crazed demon beyond the cave. No atheists in a war, they say. Precious few in a hurricane at sea. Dear God, please God, oh God. Retch. Easy to feel the world is against you at times like that. Primitive. Survival. Elements.

A hurricane. Lightning. A blood moon. The sky falling on our heads. It's in our blood. An island race. Britannia rules the waves. Filled with the sea. Our language, the salt of the Navy, barnacled idioms. Brass monkeys. Three sheets. High and dry. All at sea. Those who weren't bed ridden with sea-sickness were on watch, four hours on, eight off. U-boats. Spot a periscope and save lives. Black on black, waves the height of cliffs, a tempest. We cursed those lazy bastards in bed all day. Men who could manage a forced march after a night of ale and dancing but were poleaxed by nothing more than water and salt. Those hours on watch. Binoculars sucking my eyes out, exposed to the elements. The bridge really was a bridge on that thing, across the whole width of the ship, jutting out into space so from my station I could see back along the length of the ship as well as out and down. Take your eyes off the sea for a second and the Captain would give you a roasting, and by Christ that man could swear. Folk swore on the farm: when a sheep kicks you in the balls it's impossible not to, but the Captain used words and phrases I could only imagine the meaning of. Wondered if Queen Elizabeth knew what was being said aboard her namesake.

Four men on watch on the bridge. Captain in the middle, two flanking him, one more at starboard, the fourth at port, eight binoculared eyes and the Captain's weathered look. I was at starboard, the emptiness of the ocean, the sea and whatever was under the surface. I stared, hoping I'd never see a periscope, that nothing would come, that if there were something, I'd see it in time. She lurched ungainly against the waves, her usual slow roll exaggerated. Every six minutes another course change, zigzagging like a drunk.

Out from Gourock at night. Everything done by the military under cover of darkness. Hanging around, last minutes letters. She was anchored off the coast for protection, Jerry bombers, so we were ferried out and came on board up that massive black hull. Like an island she stood, blocking the horizon. 'No way that thing floats,' someone said. 'No fucking way that thing moves.'

The Titanic was made of metal and stone. Tiger Moths are canvas and wood.

Pitch and roll with the swell of the sea. She's floating. She's moving. Welcome aboard, and Devine, you're on guard duty.

I relieved the Yank, who handed me a machine gun. 'See this space here, buddy? Anyone wants to board through here, shove this in their face and tell him to fuck off. Everyone comes on over there, where you came on.'

It was a shell door, about six feet off the sea. 'Who's going to come from down there?'

'Some of the crew are on twenty-four hour leave, but most'll be back late. One more glass, one more trick. They'll come up here so they don't get caught. You're to stop em, right?'

'Do I shoot them?'

'Best not to. Ever used one of these?'

'Never.'

'Well, let's keep it that way.'

Scan left, right, near, far. Looking for unnatural geometry. The straight line. Should be fine, at full steam she could outrun any U-boat. Soon be out of range, closer to America than to Europe. A four day crossing. Dry land. Those boys in the U-boats though, by Christ. Rather them than me. They can have the ocean, I was going to the New World. America.

The dark streets and bright lights, the smoky clubs and smoky girls, Glen Miller, Duke Ellington, Cab Calloway, a mythical world that came through the wireless. It was mythical, yet I was on a boat heading towards it. The wild west. Of course, we might be going to Canada. I thought about Canada. Nothing. An hour of my watch left. I closed my eyes against the binoculars and could feel sleep coming. Snap out of it. A few hours into that first guard duty, as we lay off Gourock, the sound of drunks trying to be quiet rolled up the hull and a rough naval head appeared. 'Hey lad, any officers about? No? Give us a hand up then.'

'Sorry, I've been told to let no-one pass.'

'Come on, out the way.'

'No. I've got orders.'

'Aye, but orders is for officers, not for the likes of us. Let us up and we'll see you all right. Extra rations. Bit of grog on the crossing. We look after our own.'

Brought the gun up. 'Best to go back down. Come up

the proper way.'

More swearing. The Navy must have their own dictionary. 'Officious little prick aren't you? Bloody pilots, poker up their arses the lot of them. Come on Jock, get out the fucking way.'

'No.'

'You planning on shooting us? No? Then get the fuck out of the way.'

I cracked the barrel against the rail, clanging in the dark. 'Fooksake, that thing could go off.' Hard look in the eye. 'Fine Jock, you win. We'll try another way. We'll remember this though. Hope you don't need for anything in the next few days.'

An hour later the Yank returned and took his gun, handed me a stick instead.

She was built for luxury, the Queen Elizabeth, but you'd be hard pushed to notice. The Navy got hold of her, retro-fitted her to match the needs of troops crossing the Atlantic. Stripped of all her finery, anything that might make us working class boys who'd never get on her in peacetime realise the fact, realise that even at sea the haves live far better than the have-nots. The cabins were kitted out with bunk beds, the floors bare. Not a carpet in sight. The wood however was beautiful. As we'd descended that first night I ran my hand appreciatively over it, feeling the smoothness, the run of the grain, until my fingers caught on something, a groove. Kilroy was here

Shook my head. There was more vandalism in the cabins. The American troops had passed their time confined below decks carving their names into the wood. A memory, Joe carving *No Pasaran* into a tree. Watch over, I entered the bunkroom, a splitting headache and a pain in my eyes like someone had held a match against them.

There was little but tension and seasickness on board. All British ships were targets but the Queen Elizabeth, the biggest and fastest ship in the merchant fleet, would be the jackpot for Jerry. All four hundred of us onboard knew it. To cap it all, we weren't allowed on deck. Too dangerous. We could get in the way or attract attention. We were trapped below, except when on duty. There was fuel to burn.

I groaned and pulled myself up again, reached under my pillow.

'You're not playing that in here, mate.'

'Dinnae worry, I'm going out.'

We weren't allowed to go up on deck but as long as we didn't get in anyone's way or get seen by a bored officer, we could wander around below deck. Some of the lads preferred to go down to the engines, listen to the roar, talk to the engineers who did all the work, made the thing go. Joe would've been straight down there, seeking out comrades. I'd found a room near the back that no-one seemed to use, a meeting room it looked like, but empty of any furniture. I figured it might be safe to use. Music practice isn't subversive so I probably wouldn't be in too much trouble if someone came along. During the day I could remove the blackouts from the portholes and look at the ocean, this time with the eyes of a traveller rather than the eyes of a watcher. I could imagine Britain receding into the distance and for some reason I felt lighter. It wasn't that I don't love old Blighty, just I never thought I'd ever get away from it. Born on a farm in the North East of Scotland, it took a war to get to Edinburgh, let alone overseas. No grand tour for the likes of me. I'd always wanted to see the Far East; that would take World War Three. But it wasn't Britain I was escaping. I'd told the Warrant Officer everything. He took off his cap. Scratched the back of his head. 'Look, mate. I'm here on me tod. Hundreds of men passing through, coming in, coming out. Us lot, Yanks, Canadians, fucking French and Poles and Christ knows who else. You think I've got time for this? If you've been up to no good in Manchester it's none of my business. That ship turning up in New York without you on it? More than my job's worth.'

He got an MP to escort me onto the launch, told him I was seasick, a coward, LMF. A truncheon in the back and then cast off.

A week out, there was no land to be seen in any direction. In my mind, as I pictured Britain getting smaller I couldn't help seeing it in darkness, burning. The last three years had been blackouts and air raids and now that's how I thought of her. A low dark shape on the horizon, hellish glow of fires, cones of searchlights, distant insect whine of Jerry bombers, crump, crump, crump.

We were never bombed at home, out in the middle of nowhere, beyond the targets on the coast, but at night you could hear the bombs falling on Peterhead, on Aberdeen, and see the damage on the rare trips into town for the pictures, the markets. That near miss in Manchester, the whistle, the silence. That burning landmass slipped behind us as we sailed and I felt relief. Guilt at that. The bombs were still coming, sleepless nights and distraught days, burning homes and streets reduced to rubble, and there I was, racing across the Atlantic to what must be the safest spot in the whole world. Ma, Da, Lizzie, all had to stay, had to face whatever was to come.

A few months and I'd be back, a proper pilot and ready to be sent up against the Luftwaffe in a Spit or a Hurricane. Then I could try to silence the ghosts, all those voices demanding justice.

I blew an F sharp, ran up and down a bit, not really playing, just warming up, slow and mournful at first, thoughts moving through my breath, sticking around the low end, improvising a tune like an old dirge on the pipes, something to play up in the heather after a battle as the claymores and the kilts lie bloody. It suited the weather, the situation, dark and sombre. I never blew hard in case a U-boat was up and listening, some sharp-eared Captain hearing *Night in Tunisia* across the water, but gently, as my mood shifted, play helping me forget, I began to move up into the higher registers, a note here, a trill there, intruding on the theme like sunlight through clouds, the balance shifted, light ran throughout like the moments before dawn. Perfectly weighted, two distinct motifs moving away from each other. The music suggested images, ice floes on the ocean, massive plates floating around and I imagined the motifs that way, floating around, and I, the player, had to choose one before it was too late and so with one final push the darker melody dropped behind the horizon, it was day and the lighter tune won. I finished on one final F sharp, two octaves up, held it, lip-trilled harmonics but ended clean, bright. That idea, the ice floes. Like me and Scotland, floating apart. But if I could move, maybe Scotland could too. Today it was moored off the coast of Europe but in a few million years, who knew where it could be? Somewhere tropical maybe, with palm trees and coral reefs. I imagined Scotland like the Hispaniola in *Treasure Island*, freeing itself from the anchor of England and sailing off to more exotic climes, all hands on deck, mountains like sails, Shetland as a rudder and me, Jack, Jim Hawkins, scrambling over the ropes, up the masts, exploring below decks. England falling over the horizon as I, onboard the RMS Queen Elizabeth, moved towards America. That ship was like a continental plate, a self-contained metal world moving between the Old World and the New. I started a new tune. One of Terry's but improvised in a bebop style, like Nathanial had taught me. As I played I fantasised they were all still with me, like it had been in Babbacombe. Doug in Rhodesia, Terry God knew where. Joe? In prison. A quick arpeggio and I left the room, tired.

You stand by your mates
    Four hours watch. Eight off.
    Straighten up and fly right, Jack. Food. Tea. Newspapers
read and reread and circulated and recirculated.
    Days passed.

Late morning, we arrived. I was cooking, bubbling. About
ready to blow. I needed off that boat. Away from myself.
Work. Action. Something. From the moment the Statue of
Liberty could be seen, all the threats and colourful imagery
the Captain could muster failed to keep us off the deck.
That skyline. Liberty. The Empire State Building minus
giant monkey. All those buildings scraping the sky, tops like
churches, like cathedrals, castles and that's what they were,
the cathedrals and castles of the wealthy, the American dream.
    Bridge, strong and graceful. The scurry of boats and ships
this way and that across the water, ferrying, carrying, moving
the people, moving the wealth. The hard angles, the human
geometry of it all, sharp and fixed, a clear victory over nature.
Smoke, black and white rising, drifting across the clear sky.
Industry at work. The harbour side was lined with waving
crowds. We disembarked, hardly a sight to inspire confidence.
Like returning from war, not preparing to go. More like
refugees than brave warriors. The seasick had yet to lose their
pallor. Yet the New Yorkers cheered us. As we attempted to
march through the crowds a woman handed me a banana. I
looked into the faces trying to see something of the America I
knew from the cowboy books and films, from the music, from
the Yanks I'd met in Britain. Some glimpses, some turns, the
voices, those accents, Satchmo, but these were real people, flat
caps, trousers held up with string and everything. Docks are
docks. This could've been Leith, Greenock, Aberdeen.

Gratitude

Much of the information about RAF training came from my grandfather, Tom Foubister. For enduring endless questions, for allowing me access to his log book and memories.

My grandmother, Marjorie, for background details, day to day life and for never letting me forget that women contributed just as much as the men.

My mother, Patricia, for passing questions and answers between Grandad and me. Without her efforts, I'd never have been able to produce anything. For this and a multitude of other debts. Adrian Searle, for years of support and encouragement; Rodge Glass, for bringing clarity and insight when I'd lost both; Judy Moir, for support, advice and patience; Vicki Jarrett for catching my many mistakes. Robbie Guillory and all at Freight for everything.

Simon Sylvester, Robert Porter and Michael Callaghan, who read the book in its various badly written and poorly proofread forms. When I get lost in the trees, I couldn't ask for better friends to show me the woods.

My father, Michael, for everything over the years. And of course my wife, Minori, for the love, the support, for dealing with a husband who wakes up at three in the morning with an idea and switches on the light to note it down, who spends much of his life in front of his laptop and who for years at a time lives inside his head playing with imaginary people.

Acknowledgements

The majority of background information on RAF life and training, and day to day existence for recruits came from my Grandfather. I also read a great deal in preparation for writing this novel, and two books in particular proved invaluable:

By The Seat Of Your Pants! Basic Training of RAF Pilots in Rhodesia, Canada, South Africa and USA during WW2. Hugh Morgan (ed.). (Newton Publishers, Kent 1990).

How It Was In The War: An Anthology. Godfrey Smith (ed.). (Past Times, London 2001).

They provided a factual base for my flights of fancy, and the anecdotes inspired a number of smaller incidents in the book. My thanks to the editors and writers involved.

By some reckoning, the Second World War started in Versailles in 1918 and ended in Warsaw in 1989. The war against Fascism is part of our collective consciousness and to attempt a list of all the cultural sources that fed into this book would be impossible. The sheer amount of writing, film, television and art about or inspired by the conflict is intimidating, but soon that will be all that remains. Everyone who fought in the Great War has gone. All too soon, the generation that fought on the beaches and on the landing grounds will join them. I hope this book may be a tiny pebble added to the memorial cairn for a truly special generation. Not the few, but the many.

Nagasaki, words and music by Harry Warren and Mort Dixon. *Straighten Up and Fly Right,* words and music by Nat King Cole and Irving Mills.

'Away! Away! for I will fly to thee,' from *Ode to a Nightingale* by John Keats 'The British Army is not fighting for the old world. If honourable Members opposite think we are going through this in order to keep their Malayan Swamps, they are making a mistake.' From *Aneurin Bevan: A Biography: Volume 1: 1897-1945* by Michael Foot